The
SERGEANT

The
SERGEANT

by DENNIS MURPHY

NEW YORK
The Viking Press
1958

PUBLISHED IN CANADA BY

THE MACMILLAN COMPANY OF CANADA LIMITED

LIBRARY OF CONGRESS CATALOG CARD NUMBER: 58-5965

PRINTED IN U.S.A. BY THE COLONIAL PRESS INC.

For my grandmother
VINNIE A. MURPHY
in appreciation of long and constant support

The
SERGEANT

Chapter One

In the Second World War Master Sergeant Callan was a hero. It was on a day in the autumn when the French countryside was fresh and delicate after a night of rain. They were in a small wood, his platoon, advancing along the sides of a road, a quiet road that was damp and grown over with grass.

In the wood it was very quiet, close and familiar. The air was sheltered and fat poles of sun, still and yellow, were spaced among the trees. The smell of leaves and grass was strong after the rain and there was a peace, an interlude in the war. The road came to a little meadow, green and plush and as small as a cup. They went down into it, and most of them were dead as they came near the bottom, and the others ran back into the wood and buried their heads in the wet leaves below the rattling of machine guns and saw in their panicked minds a picture of the meadow, and how green and small it was.

Master Sergeant Callan had run with almost the

first burst. He was thirty-six years old then, twenty years a soldier, and he had thought so much of war, planning for it, dreaming its sounds and colors, that when the firing came it was an expected thing, long waited for, a startling answer to the silent rhythm that had built inside him. He ran back up the short green slope, moving with his arms and chest, the bullets plopping into the soft earth around him. His stomach was light with a readiness to laugh for he was sure a bullet would rip the small of his back. He reached the wood and flung his face into the leaves.

His stomach began to tighten and he was frightened in a better way. There were others around him, younger soldiers who whimpered. Carefully, he moved so that he could see through the trees. The little cup of a meadow was bare to the sun and just ahead. From its far side the machine guns were still firing. He thought that it sounded as if there were two guns. The smell of leaves and grass was gone. The whimpering of the soldiers made him feel clean, almost pure.

He began to edge backward with his knees and elbows, not thinking at all, and then he was up and running low, back down the grass-covered road. He ran until he had counted five, then he cut back into the wood, parallel to the meadow, flowing through the trees like a wild boy, body balanced out in front, the weapon low and quiet in his palms. In the wind of his running there was a motionless feeling for the rifle, a cool glow that hovered at his navel. As never before he felt tall, growing taller.

He swung again to the left, never breaking his
stride, remarkably sure that he was measuring the
meadow. Then he could see it through the trees,
a glimpse of its sudden green slope. He ran with
the green at the corner of his eye through the
trees, and then he swung for the last time to the
left. He was over on their side now, from where
the firing had come, over on the side of the enemy,
the Germans, the strangers, and he was growing
toward them and knowing he could never slow or
become cautious, knowing they were close and
then closer, feeling them like a flush of music, and
he was firing as he burst from the undergrowth,
firing before he saw them, and they were there as
he knew they would be, the snail-shell helmets
tucked in toward their guns, in two huddled groups
on each side of the road, the first group raked dead
before the others had turned. He followed his firing, almost sorry they had not seen him sooner,
wanting to plunge into them bodily. They were all
hit but one who broke feeble and ran and the
sergeant came on like a bull, dropping the empty
gun, mad to touch one alive. And then he reached
out and had the German's neck, running alongside him with the head and neck tucked under
his armpit, and they galloped together like crazed
animals until finally he twisted and they fell into
the leaves and as he choked the man the smell of
leaves and grass came back strong again, with all
the pain and joy he felt bunched into the crook of
his arm as it labored and choked and labored and
choked.

For a long moment afterward he lay by the dead
German. He got so that he was very peaceful. He
lay there terribly quiet, watching the silent blue
sky through the holes in the trees.

He took the medal, the Distinguished Service
Cross, and placed it in a cloth sack at the bottom
of his foot locker. From camp to camp, from year
to year, he rarely thought of the time he had been
a hero. Though sometimes he did. That was when
he was quite drunk. When he was quite
drunk it would become an obsession with him, not
a thing to talk about, but a feeling, a feeling that
was gently heated in his chest. If it came on while
he was drinking with other men their talk would
fade into the distance. He would be stiff in his
chair, sitting there short and square and thick, the
tough skin of his face slightly red. Their talk would
fade into the distance and he would crawl into himself, back to the dipping slope of the meadow. He
could sit transfixed in a crowd of people. It was not
the thought of those moments. It was the feel of
them. So secret and personal. Like the morning
warmth of bed.

Chapter Two

A few kilometers from Bordeaux, on the highway going north, an arrow-shaped sign pointed down a long dirt road toward the camp. It was lettered in black: CAMP LANDE DE BERNOD. Only on Army directories or road signs was it referred to like that. The men stationed there called it simply "Bernod."

It was not a pleasant place. It was built on land that had been reclaimed from marshes, and it stood on packed sand, a little higher than the surrounding meadows, a group of naked wooden buildings, cold, like a construction camp made to be abandoned. Around it the pastures and meadows spread soft and green. Water hung in little pockets beneath the grass and the mosquitoes hovered close to the earth like a fog.

There was one area that was cleared and dry; that was the petroleum depot that began at the outskirts of the buildings, fifty acres of fenced in land on which gasoline and oil were stacked in great pyramids of dark barrels. The depot was the

reason for the camp. During the day the men
would work among the barrels, stack them, re-
arrange them, clean them, guard them. It was not
often that their appearance was that of soldiers.
They wore clothes for the work, unstarched fatigues
that were wrinkled and soiled black in the creases
with oil. In leisure hours dust from the depot was
like a powder on their faces.

Perhaps a thousand men were stationed there.
They had a joke about themselves; if you were
good for nothing you were good for Bernod and
the Quartermaster Corps. But it was a true joke,
for most of their records showed a defect of some
kind, advanced age or an old wound, low intelli-
gence or bad eyes. It seemed that they had been
purposely sifted into the service units, the Quartermaster. It was hard for the good men among them,
the young draftees, the occasional sharp noncom,
for there was a tiredness over the camp, a stale
air of not caring.

The quarters of the different companies looked
much alike. Each company had a street of its own,
perhaps a hundred yards long and the whole length
humped fat with gravel to ward off the rain. Lining
the streets were slightly raised sidewalks made of
wooden planks. Tar-papered huts stood in rows behind the sidewalks and four or five men slept in
each of them. It rained in all the seasons. The
water would roll off the gravel and down into the
gullies under the sidewalks, and in heavy rains it
splashed like wharf water in the space beneath
the huts.

In wet weather there could be winds that reamed the huts hollow like lost mountain cabins. The men bunched together in the warmth of the post theater or enlisted men's club, the two official places of entertainment. Even in heavy storms the whir of the little projector in the theater could be heard from the outside, steady, regular, purring. Cigarette smoke hung through the inside darkness and the air was close and warm, and the men sat on straight-backed auditorium seats.

In the enlisted men's club it was sweaty. Two soldiers in T-shirts served beer in cans from behind a wooden plank bar. The beer was stored for everybody to see in red Coke machines full of ice. The walls of the club were of thin unfinished wood and outside the storm would rage loud, but within the voices of the men were louder than the storm, and the tables were littered with empty beer cans, and the men held full cans loosely at their sides as they tilted back in their chairs, or held them tight in front as they hunched forward over the tables. They made their own heat, and they drank bareheaded, their armpits moist, and their temples glistened white where their caps had pressed all day.

If they drank enough beer, sometimes they would leave the club and walk through the rain to the French village down the road. It was only a ten-minute walk, and because it was so close the village had been changed by the soldiers. They drank and fought in the mud of the little public square. They were superior, aggressive, mocking,

and at first the French people had only watched,
bitter. But in the years after the war they hardened.
Clumsily, in a peasant's way, they became calcu-
lating. The face of the town began to change. In
the front parlors of the stone houses rickety bars
were set up and cognac was sold by the shot. Con-
cession stands for jewelry and trinkets appeared
around the public square. A money changer from
Bordeaux came to live in the little hotel.

It got so that the soldiers paid for their superiority. And when they came in from the rain to the
parlor of a house they could expect only the cognac,
no word or warmth from the man who served it.

And when the rains ended they would not leave
the surrounding country fresh. It was beautiful,
but not clean. The sun splashed a gentle yellow
into the meadow; in twilight it was gold and still
and the air was fuzzy in the stillness, almost humming, and the puffed earth of the meadow was
velvet. To the west was a range of dark mountains,
but before the mountains was a wood of pine trees,
trimmed-looking and with a haze above their crest.
A man could stand at the edge of the camp and see
it all, the green meadow, the wood, and then the
soft mountains. Whores waited in the pine trees.
In first evening darkness soldiers filtered through
the meadow and paid for them wet on the needled
earth. The whole wood had a strange life of its own.
Three old Frenchmen, all thin and wrinkled, sat
beneath the trees and sold quarts of wine from
their knapsacks. Their customers were soldiers from

the camp, quiet men mostly, who came alone after dark and drank by themselves.

Country girls were the whores who waited. Their faces were parched and their calves blue-veined and muscled from a year or two ago of labor on the farm. They moved like shadows in the night, calling gently to approaching figures, their voices hushed in urgency; like soft birds came their cry, "Boy boy, here boy, here . . . Me no sick, boy, me no sick." Sometimes they would lift their dresses in the moonlight and spread themselves to show.

There were times when young soldiers, boys, returned with a whiteness on their faces that brought roaring laughter from their hut mates. Amid the jokes and laughter a boy would smile at himself, meekly. Though later as he lay on his cot his eyes would stare upward, unseeing, vacant.

It was autumn again and seven years from the war when Master Sergeant Callan came to the camp. He came by train to Bordeaux and he arrived in the morning when it was still dark. He went through the empty station to the street outside and a truck was there waiting. The driver, a colored private, hunched sleepily over the wheel as they rode out into the country.

Master Sergeant Callan sat high and stiff on the canvas seat. Through the side window, without turning his head, he watched the motion of the land. Morning was seeping into the black, soft spots of gray that fattened and joined into light.

The French countryside had started to shape itself, the farmhouses square against the beginning light, fences rising thin and weird between the pastures. As they drove, the dawn spread and the land took color—a cold brown in the westerly hills and black green in the thick vineyards off the sides of the road. The sky bloated white to show there would be no sun that day.

They drove in silence. The colored driver stepped up the speed, like a horse to the smell of the stables. "Juz a few minutes now," he said. He began to hum but then he paused. "It ain't much of a place, Sergeant."

The sergeant watched from the window without answering. As they drew closer to the hills he could see the outline of the camp. He could see the naked buildings and, beyond, a stretch of meadow, and then the pines and then the hills.

There was a sentry shack at the road turning into the camp and a white-helmeted soldier leaned from its door and motioned them through. They bumped along a road creviced from rains past a cluster of large wooden buildings, then on into the living area with its rows of huts and gravel streets. The driver stopped at the mouth of one of the streets, across from an Orderly shack with an orange sign over the door: 61ST PETROLEUM SUPPLY CO.

"This here's the one," he said.

The sergeant looked at him briefly then stepped down from the cab. He went to the rear of the truck and slid out his duffel bag, hoisting it clear of the road. With an almost imperceptible jerk of his head he signaled to the colored driver, turning away with his back to the truck until it started and moved off.

It was not yet full light and he stood quietly for a moment beside his bag. The company street stretched out empty. From a low building at his right issued the clang of pots and pans and with the breakfast noises came the smell of frying bacon, pungent through the morning cold. A shadowy line of men were shuffling into the building.

On the other side of the street a light showed from the window of the Orderly shack. He shouldered his bag and crossed to where he could see through the lighted window. A young soldier sat tilted near a coal-burning stove and for a while the sergeant watched him. Then he lowered the bag from his shoulder and leaned it against the shack, softly, so there was no sound.

He went around past the door of the shack and looked down the two rows of drab tar-papered huts. A gray vapor rolled off their roofs. He followed the wooden sidewalk and stopped at the first of the huts, pushing open the door with his foot. The interior was deserted. The stove at the center of the room had been left active and the unmade bunks showed a hasty departure to breakfast. He stood by the open door and after a backward glance he stepped inside to the stove, taking a thin stick from the woodbox and thrusting it down into the coals. He lit a cigarette from the ember on the stick, his eyes squinting over the

room. Against each wall there was a steel cot and
at the head of each cot a wall locker. From the top
of an open locker he brought down the framed
photograph of a girl, reading the slanted inscrip-
tion. For a moment he held the picture loose in his
palm and he grunted slightly as he replaced it.

Outside, he went down the street to its end, to
the edge of the meadow, then turned and came
back up the other side. The soldiers were beginning to return from breakfast and they looked at
him curiously as they passed on the sidewalk. He
went by them without a glance, his face red from
the cold but without expression.

When he entered the Orderly shack the young
soldier was still tilted in his chair. The office was
small, with two vacant desks facing across the stove.

"Morning," said the soldier, a corporal, a boy
only.

Sergeant Callan nodded. For a moment he looked
at the boy, who was pimpled from the underlip to
the chin. "You the company clerk?"

"I sure am." The corporal smiled with a practiced air of confidence.

"What's your name?"

The boy let down his chair and sat straighter.
"Say, can I help you?"

The sergeant moved past him toward the stove,
a silent hand extended to its warmth. He glanced
about the office, his fingers moving against the
heat.

"Can I help you, Sergeant?"

He continued to scan the room. "I'm reporting,"

he said. Then he turned suddenly toward the boy, a quick smile on his tough-skinned face, an expression that masked rather than exposed him. "My name is Callan. Master Sergeant Callan."

"Oh, you're the new first sergeant." The corporal stood up, reorganizing his behavior.

Sergeant Callan took a folio of records from inside his OD jacket. He laid them carefully on the desk away from the boy.

"Captain Loring isn't in yet, but he should be here any time. The company's out at the mess hall and I'm just kind of holding down the fort. Would you like some breakfast, Sergeant? Or if you want I can help you get your gear squared away. Hut number five is where the NCOs are sleeping."

"What have you got the light on for?" He spoke abruptly, as if to check the flow of words from the corporal, as if they were insulting. The corporal crossed the room quickly and snapped off the light. "What's your name?"

"Cowley. Corporal Cowley, sir."

"I'm a master sergeant in the United States Army. You don't call me sir."

"Yes. That's right." The corporal poked nervously at his stomach.

"Are they all like you?"

"How do you mean?"

The sergeant shook his head at the plank floor and made a sound of false wonder. He pulled a chair out from one of the desks and sat down.

Outside, three or four trucks were pulling up at the mouth of the street and men were leaving the huts to gather around them in small groups. Some of them clambered on, anxious for good seats. The sergeant sat by the stove without speaking to Cowley.

"It might be a little while before the captain gets here. Usually he gets in just after the men have gone out to the depot."

"All right."

"If you want some breakfast I could go see the cook about it. Or maybe the two of us could get your gear squared away? It might be half an hour before he comes."

"I'll wait," he said. "You don't worry about me, Corporal Cowley. You just see if you can't relax."

The corporal agreed with a rapid nod. He went to his desk and shuffled noisily through the drawers. After a bit he sat doing nothing, waiting in silence with the sergeant.

Captain Loring came in ten or fifteen minutes later, the screen door banging as he entered. When he saw the sergeant he paused, uncertain by the door, and then a dawning recognition eased his thin, middle-aged face. He came forward with a prepared pleasantness, waving off a salute. "Master Sergeant Callan, isn't it?" He offered his hand. "We've been expecting you."

The sergeant had not stood up until the captain was nearly across the room. When he had entered and paused by the door he had remained in his chair, solidly, watching, as if the man could be known in that first unguarded moment. He had seen the temporary uncertainty, the pause to form an attitude, and when he stood up to shake the officer's hand he did not smile.

"We're certainly happy to see you, Callan. Two months without a first sergeant is no play-day." He smiled genially as he spoke and the sergeant continued to regard him until their hands separated. The officer cleared his throat, smiled, and patted the desk. "Well now," he said.

They were about the same age. The officer's face was brown, the skin loose and deep with a faint glow to it. There were thick creases down his cheeks, yet his cheekbones were high like an Indian's and his face narrow. His eyes had a strained, wet brightness. "And how was the trip from the States?" he said.

"The trip wasn't bad, sir. My records and orders are behind you on the desk."

"Ah, yes." His fingers tapped along the desk top. "Maybe we should take a look at them, eh?" He laughed for no apparent reason and then glanced over at the clerk, Cowley. "Morning there."

"Good morning, sir."

"Yes, humm," he said, and he followed the tapping of his fingers until he was behind the desk and seated. He brought the record folder in front of him and looked up as if to reaffirm the sergeant's presence. "Oh, sit down, please. I don't see why we should be so formal."

The sergeant seemed to wait but then he took a chair from the side of the desk and seated himself. Captain Loring paused significantly before he opened the service record. Then he began to turn through its pages. Occasionally he made comments or a little humming sound, as though it were impolite to detach himself completely. "Yes, yes. The old Forty-first, I remember that outfit . . . humm. A lot of infantry, eh? . . . Ah, you've been in France before." When he read the citation for valor he nodded and repeated the letters "DSC."

When he had finished with the records he replaced them in the folder and set it carefully in front of him. "That's very impressive." He stared up at the opposite wall and cleared his throat. He seemed to be sobered, changed by what he had read. There was a movement of the thick crease down his cheek, as though he were in the midst of an effort, rehearsing himself. "You've had a lot of infantry. At Bernod, of course, it isn't the Infantry." He hesitated, as if he'd said a distasteful thing, as if he were on the wrong track. "I'm an old soldier myself," he began again, "believe it or not. I was in the ranks a long time before I got this commission and I don't mind telling you that either. Why should I? It's something to be proud of. Ten years an enlisted man in the Infantry. It seems like a long time ago. A man can forget, I suppose."

Evidently it was what he had wanted to speak of, for his voice had relaxed into the peculiar tone of reminiscence and he turned toward Sergeant Callan, turning as to one who would understand, a man whose record showed him admirable. "Ten years," he repeated and his eyes had the soft light

of a confession. All the gentleman's talk, his cap-
taincy—all that was acquired, a little false, and at
heart he was still with the ranks, a common man,
and his eyes with their wet brightness were willing
to reveal that now, quickly, for here was a soldier,
a man of his own age and feeling.

The sergeant took a cigarette from his breast
pocket and wet it with his tongue, watching the
officer as he lighted it. Captain Loring waited and
when he saw that his sentiments had been ignored
he looked away, embarrassed.

"It isn't the Infantry," said the sergeant, "but
that doesn't make any difference as far as running
a company goes."

"No, of course not, you're right. It's the same
job in all the branches." He smiled again, almost
anxiously. "You have a fine record and I suppose
there's not much new that I can tell you. The
most important thing though is to keep these men
from getting too lax, getting to feel like they're
just ordinary laborers. They get that impression,
I imagine, with all the routine. They've got to remember that they're soldiers." He looked for a
sign of confirmation from the sergeant. "I'm lucky
to have a man like you," he said. "Corporal
Cowley and I have been carrying most of the load
together and of course I haven't been able to be
around all the time. A good deal of time I've had
to spend on other things, duties on a post level,
you know."

The sergeant inhaled slightly, then laid his cigarette in the ash tray between them. "It's a pretty sad-looking outfit," he said.

The captain's liquid eyes widened and for a moment he appeared poised above his seat. But then his shoulders eased and he perched forward, nearly apologetic. "Well, yes, perhaps it seems that way. It's not the Infantry, I suppose that's obvious. We have a lot of trouble keeping these outfits up to par. It's mostly maintenance work they do, you know."

"The huts are plain dirty, floors dusty, bunks made loose. The company area is littered with trash, the men are walking around half in uniform, half out. I could see all that in ten minutes this morning."

"You have a very critical eye, Sergeant."

"I don't believe you hold company formations, do you?"

"We have in the past, but you know how it is with these maintenance outfits. We just didn't see the need of it."

"Who is we?"

The captain sat back in his chair. "Now just a minute, Sergeant. This has gone far enough." His eyes averted to a side window. He seemed to be straining toward a proper reprimand. "You can't expect to come in here and tell me how to run my company."

From the other desk came the quick tap of Cowley's typewriter, a politeness in the silence of the room. The sergeant remained impassive in his chair

and it was the captain who spoke again, his voice
hurt, suddenly inevitable. "It's not the easiest job
in the world. Everybody expects something, the
men on one side and then you get it from the brass
too, like you're just a robot with no feelings, just
a machine that does a job, and if you make a mistake, just one, then they all jump on you. You're
supposed to be perfect, I guess. They never think
that you've got the same feelings as any man, no,
you're just supposed to keep them closed up. You
don't know how a place like this can get a man
down."

The tap of the typewriter stopped. After a bit
the sergeant nodded, nodding without looking at
the officer, a steady motion of his head that fitted
the tempo, the wake of the revelation. He smiled
for the first time, a half-smile, and his eyes were
curious and interested. He bent forward over the
desk, openly, moving closer to the captain until he
could smell the odor of stale alcohol. It was a gesture done slowly and with precision, and the deep
skin of the captain's face loosened and his hands
on the folder were quiet in acceptance. "It's hard,"
the captain said softly.

Sergeant Callan stood up and as he glanced
about the office he pulled his OD jacket down
tight over his belt. The clerk was bent self-
consciously over his typewriter. "Yes, it's hard, I
imagine," he said. "Now I've been running companies for over fifteen years. I don't see why we
should have any trouble with this one. Suppose

you let me handle the company, since it's probably only a headache for you with your other duties. Just let me handle it how I see fit and of
course you'll have the final say in things."

The captain answered quickly, grateful, responding as to a reprieve. "Well it's no easy job keeping
an eye on a dozen things at once. The only officer
and no first sergeant for two months, just me and
Cowley running it together. I'll have the final say,
of course."

"Certainly."

"You're the kind of man I can have confidence
in," he said.

From where he stood the sergeant studied the
officer, flatly, like a child with a toy gone boring.
He moved away to Cowley's desk, watching over the
clerk's shoulder until he began again to type.

Captain Loring was left alone to their backs.
His head dropped slightly forward and there was
a subtle longing to his appearance, as if he could
start everything fresh, begin the interview anew.
He stood up slowly and went to the door. "Then
I'll be in this afternoon," he ended, and he had
to leave without a reply from the sergeant, who
remained behind Cowley until the boy turned
around in his chair.

"You're some pair, aren't you?" The sergeant's
mouth dipped with a faint disgust. But then he
laughed. His cheeks took on the redness of sudden
good feeling. He seemed quickly and strangely elated.
"Now I'll tell you what you should do," he said,
and his voice was slow and tight. "You should make

out a memorandum and post it. A memorandum
informing the men in this company of a formation
at, oh, let's say eighteen-hundred hours. Do you
think you can do that?" He smiled down at the
boy. "You can do that, can't you, Cowley?"

Chapter Three

The men knew of his arrival long before the formation. In the raw yet patterned atmosphere of the camp it was the kind of knowledge that approached the instinctive. It was enough to see a fully uniformed sergeant on their street in the early morning. Out at the depot they talked knowingly. "That's him all right, I knew the minute I seen him, that's the man."

After returning in the trucks for noon chow they crowded around the Orderly room. The clerk came out and walked through the group to tell them the new first sergeant didn't want a crowd around the office. It was a message for them all, but he came up to them singly, person to person. "It's not me. He says you gotta move on."

As they dispersed they strained to look into the shack, muttering among themselves as they went off toward the mess hall. "Tough guy . . . takin over already." But they spoke more to dull their curiosity than to complain.

When the evening meal was over they gathered

in the company street. At six o'clock he came out of the office and walked down the wooden sidewalk. They were already quiet as he approached, forming their lines without an order, but even when he was opposite them he waited, as if it could become more quiet. He stood on the sidewalk and waited, his square face alive, ready, responding to the thickness of their thoughts. And when his voice sounded they did not anticipate its force. "Comp-ny . . . tensh . . . hut!" It came loud and powerful, controlled, with a fiber of years of command. Its echo hung over their stiffness. Then it became very still. The faraway noises from the rest of the camp seemed unreal.

"I called you out here for a purpose. I am your new first sergeant. My name is Master Sergeant Callan. I called you out here because it's best we understand each other from the beginning." His clear voice was the only thing in the softness of the twilight. He paused and they stood rigid as he looked over the ranks, at their heads, the high white temples. "You've gotten along without a first sergeant. You've gotten used to having things your way. That will change. As of now that will change. You can expect three formations a day. You can expect a daily inspection of quarters. You can expect to conduct yourselves as soldiers. At ease!"

They shuffled into at-ease position, hands nervous behind them.

Then the quality of his voice changed, lower, like that of a man in idle conversation. It had an unreasonable gentleness. "Captain Loring has been occupied with other duties and he hasn't been able to devote much time to you. Perhaps that's made you careless. Perhaps you think that because you're a maintenance outfit you're not subject to the common rules of military discipline. You're wrong," he said quietly. "For example, none of you will ever again appear at a formation in a uniform like this." He reached out and grasped the soiled fatigue shirt of a soldier in the front rank, not looking at the man, but pulling the shirt out away from his body for them to see. "Most of you work in the field, I know that. But there is no excuse for this kind of filth. If you have to, you will change your fatigues daily. The man whose shirt I am holding is restricted to the company area for two weeks."

He turned away and walked slowly down the front rank. They could hear the sound of his boots crunching over the gravel, and then a silence, as if he were listening to their tenseness. "Am I understood!" His voice boomed and echoed through the street and meadow and he lingered there in the echo, his breathing deep through his tight shirt, waiting, seeming almost to weave with the rhythm of the silence. He walked again, a foot or two away from the front rank.

As he paced down the line the men tightened inwardly, nervous with the feel of him, vaguely ashamed. They could feel him on the surface of their skins. He paced down the line and like a shadow they could feel his gaze passing over their bodies.

In the front rank there was a soldier who was straighter, stood taller than the rest. He was young and his good-looking face was clean, bright, and his tallness in the rank was easy and unstrained. There was a separateness about him, perhaps the uniform, which was washed into a faded gray, or perhaps the cool brightness of his face in the twilight. He seemed to stand alone, distinct.

The sergeant passed slowly down the line and when he saw the boy his eyes flicked quickly away. Then he turned back, looking him up and down, slow and thorough, as if to atone for his turning away. Carefully, he confronted him. "What's your name, soldier?"

"Private First Class Tom Swanson." The boy spoke evenly, unafraid.

The sergeant hesitated. He hovered there, his stance firm, yet he seemed to move, to rock slightly on the heels of his feet.

"How long you been in this outfit?"

"Eight months."

"Where do you work?"

"In the field," said the boy.

Again he hesitated. But he seemed locked, stiff, as if to turn away would be weakness. "What are you so proud about?" he said.

The boy did not answer. The sergeant stood in front of him, hands stiff at his sides. His head inched forward as if to demand a response but then some inner control apparently checked him. He stayed a moment longer, his lips tight, then wheeled abruptly and walked back to where he faced the company. He let them go with a few words and a curt "Dismissed," preoccupied, rather strained as by an anti-climax, and as they broke off into straggling groups he watched from the sidewalk, following the long strides of the tall boy in the faded uniform.

Chapter Four

When Tom Swanson left the formation he did not loiter with the others on the street but went directly to his hut, picked up a towel and clean underclothes, then walked down to the showers. The showers were in another hutlike building at the edge of the meadow. He was alone as he undressed and stepped beneath the hot water. He could feel the grime of the depot rolling off his body, sifting away with the vapors of steam.

Every time it was new, these minutes in the shower, fresh and new, filled with a slow anticipation. He anticipated the next instant of hot water and he anticipated the evening ahead. It was almost a ritual to come here before going on pass. The cleanness after a day's work, that was one thing, but it was more, alone there in the shower room, like living a little ahead of himself.

He ran a towel over his shoulders and thought of the new sergeant. When the man was standing before him there had been a kind of nervousness, a vague lifting in his chest. It was an uncomfortable

feeling. But he smiled as he dried himself. That was
one tough sergeant if ever there was one. He could
hear the men talking in the company street. They'd
be all night talking about him. He could hear it
perfectly.

"I tell you, he ain't nothin but a sonofabitch.
What else can yuh say about a guy like that? A
sonofabitch, period. Just when I seen him comin
' out of the Orderly room, just the way he walked,
right away I knew the story. I could tell the first
minute, lookin at yuh the way he does, struttin
around like a goddamn king!"

And when they talked about the sergeant there
would be a little awe too, reluctant, but stronger
in its reluctance.

"But he's a stocky little guy. Did yuh see the
campaign ribbons?"

"Ribbons don't mean nothin. Not in runnin
an outfit like this."

"Yeah, but yuh gotta hand it to him. He's kinda
cool actin."

He finished with the towel, still smiling at the
voices in his mind. Part of it was amusement with
himself, his inclination to live over scenes without
actually being there. But that's the way it would
be, he was sure.

When he'd gotten into the crispness of his
shorts and T-shirt he sat for a moment in the warm
room. He took some deep breaths and closed his
eyes. He was happy and he knew it then. The camp
was the worst place in which he'd ever been and he

was happy and he felt lucky about it. He thought again of Sergeant Callan. He would be the kind of man who would make changes in the company, perhaps change the policy on passes. It wasn't a good thing to think of because he was feeling fortunate. Yet in the company he was probably the only soldier who took regular passes. They were easy enough to have but none of the others took them. Sometimes he knew why, knew what it was they felt. There was a security to the camp, a home and a familiar idle sadness. Going on a leave or pass to Bordeaux was a change, a break that brought a fresh and different unhappiness. At the camp they could stay quiet, cocoon-like. He knew men who gorged themselves at evening chow so that they would sleep soon, so that they could return to their huts and lie fully clothed in a warm and bloated sleep. He knew. Occasionally he had fallen into it himself.

He remembered a conversation one night in the recreation room. He had listened with that peculiar awe of having heard it before but understanding for the first time. "You know, it's funny," a man was saying over pool, "it's gettin so I can't sleep all night with a woman. No, listen, it's funny. Last week I was in Bordeaux, in bed with this woman see, and goddamn if I didn't jump up in the middle of the night and come back here." As the man spoke he had laid down his cue stick and was urgent with what he was saying. "I felt nervous right there in bed. You know what I mean? Like being away I was doin somethin wrong."

But Swanson didn't want to think too much about the other men. As he sat there he was still warm with the fortunate feeling. If the sergeant wouldn't change the policy on passes, that was the important thing. He could feel again, quickly, the closeness of Callan's face, red and square and close.

In his shorts and T-shirt he walked back to the hut. There was nobody there except Sam, who lay in his shorts on the bunk. Sam was rotund and hairy and had white friendly arms. He watched as the boy began to dress out of his locker.

He wore civilian clothes when he took his passes, sport jacket, shirt, and slacks, all of which he had bought in Bordeaux out of his first overseas pay. The slacks were cut thin in the French manner. At first he had been embarrassed wearing them but now whenever he put them on he felt a beginning joy.

"I swear, I don't know how you do it," said Sam. He watched Swanson with a look of amused admiration. "I swear, night after night. Don't you ever stay home? What's wrong, don't you like us fellows in the barracks? I bet you got yourself a little French chick." He spoke in a rapid, familiar way, a little forced, enough to show that he was not really familiar with the boy.

Swanson combed his hair into the mirror on the inside of the locker, smiling. "Well, I don't know." He looked over at the other man, who spent most of his free time in his shorts on his bunk. "You should get out once in a while, Sam. It's a great feeling."

"Too much trouble," he said. "And I ain't picked up that lingo like you. Jesus, how'd you pick it up so good. Just like a frog."

Then with the sudden vividness of the lazy he sat up. "How about that new sergeant? Huh? He sure as hell jumped on you."

"Yeah, I guess he did."

"Jesus, why'd he do that? He didn't have no call to do that."

Sam waited, perched on his bunk, but the boy did not look over from his locker. "You know, it was just because you was standin there tall like a soldier and it made him steam. He's gonna make it tough all around, that guy. I seen a lot like him and I can tell you he's got a mean streak."

"You might be right."

"I hear he got the DSC," said Sam, and then he lay back on his bunk, as if he were embarrassed at having said it.

"He's probably a pretty good soldier," said Swanson. He put the comb back into the locker and shut it. "Anyway, I'll see you in the morning." He waved over at the man as he left the hut.

He had to go into the Orderly room to pick up his card from the pass box. It disturbed him to think he had to stop there. Already he was feeling the warm surge, the start of the evening. He didn't want to see the new sergeant.

But he had to pick up his pass card and when he entered the office he took it quickly from the box and signed his name in the overnight ledger, all without looking at Callan, who was sitting alone at

the far desk. As he wrote his name he could feel
the man watching him. When he laid down the
pencil he turned, against his will, and nodded.

Callan was watching him from behind the desk,
the blue eyes steady. "Going out, Swanson?"

"Just to Bordeaux." He was surprised at the
sheepishness of his voice. He remained a moment
longer but the sergeant made no other sign and
as he left the office he went down the road half
ashamed of himself.

But the road into Bordeaux was a ritual too, no
place to be thinking of anything. There was still a
bit of light, enough to spread a stillness before the
cold rustle of night and he walked until the camp
was small back in the distance. The vineyards on
each side of the road stretched into a deep purple.
He had no feeling of hurry but the old, gentle excitement had begun and he wanted to keep walking. He let several cars pass before he stopped to
hitch-hike. And even hitch-hiking was a game, a
great concentration, an effort to stop each car with
his mind. One passed. Then a Citroën stopped and
he was laughing with himself as he stepped in next
to a fat Frenchman. The Frenchman boomed jovi-
ally, "Et alors, mon vieux!"

Coming into the city the road widened into four
lanes of cobblestone. Buildings began to grow on
either side, dull-colored structures two or three
stories high, the lower portions alive with little
businesses, *pattiseries, boulangeries,* the upper
stories drab recesses from the vitality beneath. Fat
women stood lazy in the doorway of the little

businesses, old shawls warm over the slope of their shoulders, their skirts black and shiny at the hips. The big street was split by a thin island of trees and children in blue short pants skirted between the cars back and forth to the island, their voices shrill, higher than the peep of horns, their giggling laughter secret with the excitement of the oncoming night.

Tom Swanson peered from the window of the Citroën. As they slowed he could see a dark-haired girl who stood alone on the sidewalk, her cheeks faintly rose in the cool. Under her tight sweater her breasts were full and pointed, but with something more, a softness to them, like an aura. He reached out, elated, and waved. He could see her turn and watch the car as it passed, acknowledging him by the way her body remained firm, only her head turning. It made him excited. He wanted to call out to the Frenchman driving the car, "That's the girl I'm going to marry! Dammit! Don't you ever feel like that? Don't you ever feel like taking something out of nowhere and it would be good, it would be pure, just because you don't know anything about it?"

He got off happy at the bridge that crossed into the city, making his way through the thickness of pedestrians, out along the bridgewalk. Halfway across he stopped and leaned over the rail, watching the river suck past brown and fat beneath him. It swirled out toward an ocean he couldn't see. Great flood walls of stone restrained its edges, and the whole length of river was lined by tin warehouses, with white sea-going vessels hugging the flood walls, rolling softly at anchor. Behind him, the passing of French voices. Then the bridge on which he stood. Out front the river, the Garonne, and the city itself, a gray depth of foreignness. Each time he was exhilarated by this strange world and the power to be friendly with it.

There was a sudden added comfort in the smoothness of the concrete of the bridgewalk. He could feel it at his feet and think of the concrete of his grammar-school paper route, a route on Elm Street, with elm trees really there, delivering papers on his bike in the late afternoon, first down one side and then the other, a fresh pride with the throwing of each paper and the sound of its thud against the wooden porches. The last house on the route was his own and it had the only concrete driveway on the street, very smooth and perfect to ride a bike on, and coming into it, the newspaper bag wrinkled empty over the handle bars, he would be gliding, a joy in the first contact with the smoothness of that concrete, standing high on one pedal, then coming down quickly and hard on the other, just once, enough to make wind and sail down the driveway into the garage. And the garage was suddenly warm and windless, on its floor an oval spot of oil, the most familiar thing he knew.

He turned and went on across the bridge down into the city, walking up the Rue Victor Hugo toward the Bar Jacque. It was seven-thirty. The street lamps came on, much as in the States. With their light the night became suddenly cooler and he

walked fast toward the little side street where
Jacque's was the only bar. Madame Jacque would
come out from the rear shouting, "Monsieur
Tom! Monsieur Tom!" loud enough so that sometimes people stopped and looked in. At first he had
gone there so he could speak French. She seemed
to understand him, nodding to everything he said,
never once a doubtful sign in her eye. When he
got going with her he felt like a Frenchman. She
was a fat, jolly woman. "Never any Américains come
into my place!" That's what she always told him.
"I've seen them in other places, understand. Les
soldats Américains! Ach! But you, you are not like
them," and her tone would slip into a mixture of
the mother and lover, "you, you are different, yes,
very nice, très très beau."

I don't give a damn about that, he would think,
yet his speaking would begin to speed up, twice
as fast, with phrases he'd never tried before, using
gestures even, and the whole while her head
bobbed vigorously with understanding.

He turned the corner and went into Bar Jacque
and she came out from the rear with her arms extended. "Monsieur Tom, Monsieur Tom!" She was
pouring from a cognac bottle before he had
reached the bar. "It's cold outside, no? So take
this." She set up the cognac, reaching across with
a fat arm to grasp his shoulder. The husband joined
them from the rear, a man half her size who never
spoke but who smiled and made a little wave as
he stood beside his wife.

"You embarrass me every time," said Swanson

in his slow French, and actually he could feel himself blushing.

"So what difference?"

"No difference."

"Et alors. Is she coming? That is what we must know. Is she coming tonight?"

"Who?"

"Who! Ah, how you speak. Don't speak to me if you say who."

"I don't know for sure. I think she's coming about eight."

"I'm glad," and she leaned across the bar and became softer. "She is exquisite. She is of class. For months I am worrying, when will this boy find a girl, this good boy who needs a good girl. And then suddenly . . . Ah."

He drank the cognac beneath the beams of husband and wife. "All right. But Solange is just a girl I've met. You can't say that we really know each other." He was speaking with a blush that had heightened and the two French people continued to beam on him and he knew that, more than embarrassment, it was some kind of crazy satisfaction that he was feeling. "All right," he said again.

"We will leave you alone," said Madame Jacque. "You go sit by yourself at that table."

He paid for another cognac and took it to the table. He was the only customer. It was a small café with just the three tables and several stools up next to the bar.

When Madame Jacque retired to the rear he tried to quiet himself, tried to empty out his

mind. But the girl who was coming blurred everything. For a moment he tried to plan out what
would happen. But it wasn't like walking into this
bar. With the girl it would make it bad if he tried
to know or anticipate it. He was excited. He just
wanted to let it come.

A little after eight she appeared. As he stood to
greet her he saw the young man who followed and
he picked up the cognac from the table, trying to
be casual with it. She came across the room smiling
openly. "Hello, Tom! I got your note this afternoon just as Paul and I were going to the cinema."

He put down the drink to shake her hand.

"I should have phoned. I didn't give you a
chance to answer."

"No, it was fine, and I like letters. May I pre-
sent you to Paul Soubrin, Tom Swanson."

He shook hands with her companion, a man
shorter than she with an amiable shininess to his
features. They stood uncertainly, like an eddy of
three among sidewalk pedestrians.

"We shall have a drink then?" asked the man
with her. "You understand French? Yes, Solange
says you do. I am not so talented as Solange, that
beautiful English! But then neither am I a student
at the University. So. I will avoid being a fool and
speak French."

"Tom understands perfectly," said the girl.
"You may talk all you please."

"Ah, that is my great pleasure."

They sat down into a period of silence after the
first strain of exuberance. He was still tight with

the disappointment of seeing her with someone else.

"Paul is my brother-in-law who is staying with us for a few days." She said it with a quick consideration that made her face innocent and tentative.

"Ah," said Paul. "She wants you to know that immediately."

Swanson smiled then, along with Paul, and the two of them looked at the girl. He looked at her now with a clean easiness, at the blondness of her, at the eyes sparkling blue with shared good feeling. Her hair came out in white wisps around the glow of her forehead and the shoulders were round and soft beneath her blouse. He wanted to reach over and put his arms around her, soft at first.

"I know all about you," said the brother-in-law to Tom. "I disapprove of everything. Garçon, three cognacs."

Madame Jacque appeared and when she brought the drinks she glanced darkly at the young Frenchman.

"I must disapprove, you see," he said. "Even that fat woman is in conspiracy. Ah yes. Tonight we have been to a movie. Boom boom boom. An American film. Randolph Scott. He makes me very happy. Do you like him, I must know. Solange says that you are very intelligent, a soldier who belongs in the University, a young man with a great heart for life." Without waiting for an answer he turned and looked about the small café. "So this is where

you had your rendezvous!" He waved his arm dis-
paragingly. "It is not much. It is not romantic."

"Paul!"

"You see," he said to Tom, "I know everything.
I am her confidant."

"Paul is not exactly my confidant," she said.
"When we came from the movie to meet you I told
him that we had been here together once before.
And I must have told him also that we met in an
outdoor café."

"Yes, that is the part I disapprove of. If your
father knew, Solange, or your mother! Ah! When
I was your age, two or three years ago, girls were
not permitted such a liberal way of life. You, Monsieur Swanson, what do you think of meeting a girl
in a café?"

"I think it's fine," he said.

"You do? And so do I. Eh bien." He finished
his glass and took a crumpled five-hundred-franc
note from his pocket, laying it on the table. "I
am leaving you with the bill paid. That is because
at heart I am really very nice."

"Don't be silly, Paul. You're not going?"

He leaned over and kissed her on the forehead.
"Little one, little one, it is a great tragedy, I
know." He turned with quick good spirit to shake
hands with Tom. "She is in your trust." He paused,
rather seriously. "She is an exceptional girl." Then
he made his way out of the café, turning once to
wave before he disappeared through the door.

And when the door had swung closed it was dif-

ferent. They sat for a time without speaking. He
had trouble looking over at her. "He's a good
brother-in-law to have," he said.

"Yes, he is."

"Does he really disapprove?"

"He disapproves of hardly anything," she said,
but there was a thinness to her voice, as if she were
repeating something remembered, as if she also
felt the sharpness of being alone.

They had never really been alone, he thought,
not with the anticipation beforehand. When he
had met her it was with a rare spontaneity, a quick
thing as they sat closely as strangers at an outdoor
café. It was easy then, turning to talk to the girl
next to him, surprised with the way their talking
had pyramided, crazily, one thought sparking another, everything becoming important and vital
because one of them was saying it. He had begun
to feel her right then. And the following afternoon, Sunday, it was easy too, walking in the
streets to Café Jacque, and Madame Jacque and
her husband close and laughing around them.

But now it was difficult. He didn't want anything unreal with her. It seemed as though it
would be unreal if he started talking just to ease
himself. He forced himself to look at her face,
and she too was turned away, nervously. It made
him suddenly lighter to see that. It made him
happy for both of them. She turned toward him
and when she saw that he was knowing her, looking at the two of them together there, she smiled

and then laughed. Her eyes were bright on the moment. "Salud," she said.

He walked her home afterward, and once, as they crossed an intersection, she moved ahead of him a bit and he could see her momentarily as something separate, a tall girl with a fine natural motion to her body, legs that were long with a brown fullness in the calves and her face in sudden profile, unaware, expectant. It was almost necessary to stand away before he could know how beautiful she was. And of the three times they had been together they had only talked. But that was all right, he thought. It wasn't an end as he'd sometimes seen it. It was a beginning. It was part of a building thing.

He watched her ahead of him and as they walked the streets became quiet and dark. They reached her house, a two-story brownstone building with a small plaque on the door, "Alfred Gerard, Médecin."

"Your father's a doctor?"

She nodded. "And my mother is what you call a housewife."

He only slightly listened. He stood alone with her in front of the house. He touched her. Softly. The palm of his hand touched her waist. Without a sound she moved next to him. He kissed her and her lips were moist, warm. The feel of her breasts was a light heat on his chest. He kissed her again. It was soft, alive, a beginning.

Chapter Five

Out at the petroleum depot it was open and bare, the earth scraped quick clean by tractor blades, freshly brown, pugnacious. There was a single yellow shack near the entrance. Then the ground spread flatly into a haze and in the distance began the endless stacks of barrels, as small as rivets in the earth. Walking toward them, one weaved around the scars of past rains, mucky dark abrasions that made the harder ground seem familiar and old, its dust a padded comfort. On clear days there was a sensual mystery to the expanse of land. It came with the sun off the dusty ground, in slow skinless balloons, yellow and grainy. It hung in the distance where little figures of men worked stiff and unreal.

It was on a clear day that Sergeant Callan came to the yellow shack. As the jeep approached, a soldier appeared at the steps of the shack and came down with his hands in his pockets, waiting until the jeep was alongside. "Morning," he said. He was a buck sergeant. He tipped his fatigue cap and stood by the fender as Sergeant Callan looked him over.

"You're in my company, aren't you?"

The soldier's old and sunburned face nodded.

"You in charge out here?"

He nodded again and cleared his throat. "You wanta look around some, Sergeant?"

The sergeant got out of the jeep and sat on the steps of the shack, gazing out toward the distant pyramids of barrels. "What would happen if a bomb was dropped in there?" he said.

"We got 'em spaced so's no one will set off another."

He turned to the soldier slowly. "That's what the officers tell you."

The soldier looked away and for a moment they lapsed into quiet. The sergeant sat on the steps, then reached down and took a handful of dust and kneaded it in his palm, watching it sift back onto the ground. "Is there a Private Swanson working for you?"

The soldier inclined his weathered face, the eyes lighting with interest. "There is. Tom Swanson." He seemed about to go on but hesitated.

"Where is he?"

"Out there. He works a crew of Frenchmen."

"Pretty good boy?"

The soldier hesitated, watching the sergeant. "He's a nice fella," he said solidly. "He ain't a smart alec like some of these young ones."

"Sounds like you're making up for him."

"I ain't doin that." The soldier appeared disappointed with himself, as if he had offered a confidence carelessly, then had it violated. "He's about my best man. A nice, soft-spoken fellah."

"Yeah? I think I'll go out and see him."

The buck sergeant nodded. "You let me lock up the shack I'll go with you."

"I can find him all right."

"There's a lot of men out there."

"I'll find him." He walked past the jeep out toward the depot, not looking back at the man.

Swanson worked with his crew rolling barrels up a wooden ramp into the bed of a truck. Three Frenchmen were on each side of the ramp, the boy at the high end, and they worked in comfortable precision, hoisting then rolling a can upward, moving together subtly conscious of each other, like the limbs of a body. They worked steadily. When the bed of the truck was loaded they stepped back one by one from the ramp, shaking themselves with satisfaction, shuffling for a moment in the slight embarrassment of a job finished well. The boy took his cap off and rubbed a sleeve across his forehead. He ran a hand through his brown hair. The work always eased him. It was midmorning, a good time of day. He stood for a moment feeling the pale sun.

Something caused him to turn quickly and he saw a man sitting half concealed by a stack of cans. The man was sitting and as he rose and came forward Swanson knew it was the sergeant. He knew it before he could properly see him. Callan walked toward them across an open space. "Hello, soldier," he said.

Swanson nodded uncertainly. The sergeant came up to the ramp and pushed down on it as if he were testing its strength. He looked at Swanson. "I've been watching you."

"Oh?"

"Uh-huh." He glanced casually at the group of Frenchmen. "You've got a good crew here. You get good work out of them."

"Thanks." He repeated the compliment in his slow French to the workers, who milled around him, shy.

"They like you too."

"We get along pretty well."

The sergeant pursed his lips and made a whistling sound, hollow. He put his hands in his belt and looked at the ground. "How old are you, Swanson?"

"Twenty."

"That's pretty young to have a crew of men."

Swanson didn't answer. He was curious. He wondered what the man had come for. The Frenchmen had moved instinctively from the conversation, talking among themselves, a light murmur.

"What's the depot sergeant's name? The fellow in the shack?"

"Sergeant Clyde?"

"You know what Sergeant Clyde said about you." He waited a moment. "He said you were a good boy. He said you were his best man."

Swanson's cheeks tightened quizzically. "That was nice of him."

"Nice of him?" said the Sergeant. "What'd you do in civilian life, Swanson?"

The boy leaned back against the ramp, as if to adjust himself to the questioning. "For a while I worked in a cannery."

"In Madera, California," said the sergeant. He allowed for Swanson's surprise, then lowered himself to his haunches, a hand playing with the dirt, watching the boy. "I been looking at your records," he said.

"Oh?"

Near where Callan sat a loose can lay on its side. It was frosted with dust and grease, a coating that had a funny, seething life under the sun. He reached out and rubbed his finger down the curved surface, making a groove through the grease. "How'd you like to work for me?"

"In the Orderly room?"

"That's right. As company clerk."

Swanson was standing above the sergeant and he went and sat on the running board of the truck, opposite him. His eyes were curious to the offer. "I don't know anything about that kind of work."

"You can learn quick enough. I've been through the records of every man in this company and no one's more suited than you."

"This is kind of surprising. I've never done anything but field work."

"Well, I'm giving you a chance."

"I appreciate that." Through the beginning confusion he searched for the right thing to say. "You've seen that Form Twenty, so you know I've never been farther than high school. Some of the men have been to college. They'd be better for that kind of work, wouldn't they?"

"Look, Swanson. When I pick a man for a job it's because I know he can handle it."

It was difficult to be relaxed with the sergeant. Swanson wanted to shake off the anxiousness and he answered quickly. "To tell the truth I like it in the depot. I've gotten used to it and time passes right along."

The sergeant squinted. "Maybe something's wrong here. I'm offering you a better job than the one you've got and you sit there fooling around. You're fooling around, Swanson."

"It's not that I don't appreciate it. I do. It's just that I think I could do better work out here."

"You're telling me you don't want the job?"

"I guess so. Yes," he added shortly, but even then it was almost apologetic. It was as if he were doing something contrary to the man himself. As if the offer of a job were a personal thing.

Gravely, Callan leaned and spit between his legs. "I'll be damned," he said. He looked up hard at the boy. "You better reorganize your thinking some." He hovered forward. "I can order you into that office." He watched Swanson, who was suddenly calmer, and as he stared at the boy his manner changed. He leaned back and his chunky body seemed to relax. He folded his arms, apparently distracted. "But I won't do that. If you don't want the job, don't take it. Nobody works for me who don't want to." He gazed out to where the mountains were a line of gray, biting his lower lip thoughtfully. "How much longer you got over here?"

"Ten months."

"Ten months. That's a long time for a young man. A long time. And the Army's no place to be independent." He turned back to Swanson, lifting a hand to stop him from speaking. "No, no, don't tell me that you're not trying to be independent. Don't try to explain anything to me. Look here." He hunched forward, his palms open across his thighs in a manner of sudden sincerity. "You can type, I saw that on your record. You're intelligent, I think I know that myself. Now I feel I need a new clerk and that you're the best man. It's simple." He paused. "It's not a thing you should turn down," he said. "Think about it a little."

"All right. It's not that I take it lightly."

The sergeant spoke again, softly. "You come to work for me, Swanson."

He seemed reluctant to end the talk. After a while he stretched himself from off the ground, looking toward the far end of the depot as though he'd forgotten the boy. "Think about it," he said. He turned and walked rapidly across the depot back toward the jeep.

That evening, when Swanson walked in from work with his crew, the depot sergeant, Clyde, came out from the shack to meet him. "You see Callan?" he asked.

"This morning," he said. "We talked for a while."

· "Yeah? Christ, he was sore when he came back here. Chewed me out for nothin. He's a tough one, that guy. What'd you do to get him sore like that?"

Swanson shrugged his shoulders. "God, it beats me." But it was some kind of pose and he knew it then as he was speaking. He handed the sergeant the two wrenches that he'd signed out in the morning. He liked Clyde better than most of the men at the camp. He didn't want to speak with him about Callan.

"What'd he want to see you about?"

"Well, nothing much. Just came to look around and talk, I guess." He wanted to be out of the depot and into the truck back to camp. He was a little ashamed talking to Clyde. He was reluctant to mention that the sergeant had offered him a job and he was ashamed of his reluctance. "See you in the morning," he said, and he walked off toward the truck.

Chapter Six

Sergeant Callan had taken a hut for his own, the hut next to the Orderly shack. The three other NCOs living there were moved out by his order.

He kept it immaculate always, its cleanness making it seem more empty. A steel wall locker, a steel foot locker, and a tightly made cot. In the middle of the room was the black, pot-bellied stove. The dust between the planks of the wood floor had been swept until the crevices were naked and cold. The wall locker was left open to show the precise arrangement of his uniforms. He had no civilian clothes. His foot locker stood open also, the soap, the comb, all the toilet articles placed symmetrically on a spread white towel. There was nothing personal to the room, nothing in the open lockers that could bring to an onlooker a quick sympathy or knowing. The colored private who supplied coal to the stove boxes came and went quickly through the hut with distaste. "A man ain't got no right to live like that," he said around the company. He said it as if he'd discovered something.

From the day of the sergeant's arrival, Captain Loring's appearances in the company became less frequent. He entered the Orderly room around nine, rubbing his hands briskly, as if it were cold outside. "Everything going fine? Everything all right, Sergeant?" He plopped himself in a chair in front of one of the two desks. "They're some things to sign I suppose. Let's see, did I get everything yesterday?" He leafed quickly through the box marked "Incoming Correspondence." "How's the cesspool, did they fix that cesspool, Sergeant?"

Callan never spoke much with the captain. He bent over the day's paper work, answering with an occasional "Yes" or "No." The less attention he showed the more ingratiating the officer became. "The company's certainly shaping up. You should hear the reports I've had! You have no idea how it eases my mind, Sergeant, having you here. I've been wondering lately how we ever got along before you came."

Usually he would be out of the office by nine-thirty. Sometimes he would return for a few minutes in the late afternoon and look quickly about, muttering small sounds of approval. "Uh-huh, uh-huh." He would leave happy, as if he'd accomplished something.

Once the sergeant followed him to the officers' parking lot. The captain was just in his car, Sergeant Callan coming around from the rear. When he got to the window the captain was taking a bottle of scotch whisky from under a coat on the seat.

"I forgot these papers, sir."

"Huh! Sergeant Callan. Oh yes, yes certainly." He had tried to bury the scotch beneath the coat but in his fumbling the effort had become ridiculous and he left it sitting open, ignoring it beside him.

"I'm sorry to bother you. If you could just sign these leave requests," said the sergeant, his head partly through the window. The captain signed the papers quickly against the steering wheel.

When he took them back, Callan lingered a moment, the scotch in full view. The captain made a little laugh.

"Thank you sir," said Callan, saluting as he turned away from the car, very serious and respectful.

Callan issued most of his orders by means of memos posted on the bulletin board outside the recreation room. On some days there would be several memos, four or five. Coming in from the depot the men would gather to read them. "Outline of Procedure," they were headed. Without passing a direct word he created a rotating guard, juggled men from their accustomed jobs, announced that Saturdays would henceforth include a half-day's normal work load. It was as if his distance were a means of power. When they were in his presence they felt him.

They avoided the Orderly room. When they

passed by on their way to the mess hall they slipped off the wooden sidewalk onto the gravel street. It was an instinctive thing. "They're scared a him, thas what," said the colored soldier who supplied coal to the stove boxes. His name was Ivy and his job moved him from hut to hut where he saw a good many soldiers and talked a great deal. "You ever seen a place so different in such short time? Don' see nobody relax no more. Jus' being around, thas all he has to do. Can't nobody relax. Ain't that right? Ain't I right?"

The soldiers half laughed at him. It was a way of easing themselves. "No, ain't I right?" he persisted, searching the faces of the more respected soldiers, men like Clyde.

"Well," said Clyde, "this outfit has needed somebody like him. You gotta say that. He's a soldier, no denyin." Clyde was a gentle kind of man, older and with a country way about him. He had been moved from his hut, along with the other NCOs, to make room for the sergeant. He hadn't minded, for his wife had been allotted a space on a transport and it was only a matter of days before she would arrive. They would live together off-post in a farmhouse he had rented. He wanted to meet his wife in Paris and one day he went in to see Callan about a three-day pass.

"You want a pass, do you?" Callan sat facing away from him.

"Yes."

"It's a nice thing to have your wife over. Isn't it?"

"I've been looking forward to it all right."

"I didn't know about this, Clyde. I didn't know you'd made these arrangements."

"Well, most of it was done before you came, Sergeant."

"What about facilities? Have you rented a house?"

"Oh yes. I've done all that. I've been working on it a long time." He was easier, warming to the subject.

"Don't you think that she could make it down from Paris by herself?"

Clyde tightened where he stood. He knew that a three-day pass was accepted procedure for men with wives arriving from the States.

"I imagine she could make it down by herself," Callan said. He stared out the window, then looked at Clyde, his forehead arched, as if seeing him for the first time. "Do you think you deserve a pass?"

"I've been waiting a long time," Clyde said slowly. "I haven't taken a pass in six months."

"I didn't ask you that. I asked you if you thought you deserved a pass."

The buck sergeant stood silent, his hands strained along his trouser seams. On Callan's face there was a little half smile, as if he were thinking of a funny story. "Sometimes you give a man a pass to meet his wife and he'll go off chasing whores in Bordeaux." He turned away from Clyde's strained face, looking once again out the window. His fingers tapped slowly on the desk top. Then he turned

back. His blue eyes were filled with a sudden innocence. "Certainly, Clyde, you take that pass. Take
it and the best of luck to you. And when your wife
gets down here we'll do everything we can to see
that she's comfortable."

Outside, Clyde went down the sidewalk half
dazed. A soldier that worked for him in the depot
greeted him and took hold of his sleeve. "You all
set?"

Clyde shook his head dumbly. He had plain features, a little slope to his nose. He was a quiet
man, kindly.

"What's wrong?"

"That s.o.b.," he whispered.

The soldier gestured toward the Orderly room,
understanding. "Him?"

"I got so I didn't even want the friggin pass."

The soldier gestured again, his lips firm. "I know
what you mean." He followed Clyde down the sidewalk. "I know what you mean all right. I tell you,
Sergeant, I got a feeling about that guy." He
pointed toward his spine as they walked. "Right
here in the backbone. I got a feeling about him."

Swanson saw him only at the formations. In the
mornings his voice shattered their sleepiness. He
was there again at noon and evenings, in freshly
pressed khakis, the commands brusque and sharp,
his eyes keen as from an inner anxiousness. His
voice would blast at them. "You think it's tough,
do you? You think because you're a maintenance

outfit that you shouldn't be disciplined like the
Infantry? Well, let me tell you that you're wrong.
You'd better know that, and know it now."

During the formations there were many silent
intervals. He had a habit of standing out in front
and looking at them through the quiet. He would
look down the rows of faces, slowly, and the quiet
would become heavy and palpable. But he never
looked at the boy. Swanson was aware of it. The
man's eyes would avoid him, skip past. It was
frightening. It seemed to make a world for just the
two of them.

"Something's not right about him," said Aldous
Brown. Aldous was a Negro about Swanson's age,
a hut mate. He sat across from Swanson on a foot
locker, heavy-hammed, his full black arms resigned
between his legs. "He seem to be tryin too hard,"
he said.

"Jesus yes," sighed Sam, and he flopped over in
his bunk so that he faced the others. "He's bad.
There ain't no doubt about that."

Aldous Brown stared through his legs down at
the plank floor. "I'm not exactly sayin that." His
brows arched as if to anticipate his own next state-
ment.

"There ain't no use philosphizin," said Sam.
"It's simple, one two three. They get that many
stripes an they think they're God almighty."

The room was filling up with the heat of the
stove. All of them were in their fatigues, except
Sam, who lay in crumpled shorts on his bunk.

With a steady circular motion of a dry cloth, Swanson polished the toes of his parade boots. He had heard barracks talk about the sergeant before, yet he listened with a particular awareness.

"It seem like he goin too fast," said the Negro.

"Well, he better not fool with me," said Sam. He turned his hairy back to the men, the crumpled shorts creasing into his soft butt. Nobody paid him any attention.

In all, four men lived in the hut. The fourth man was Pop Henneken. He sat dumbly on his foot locker, staring out at the stove. He was a private first class, the lone chevron on his sleeve like the little roof to a house, for below it was a dark area that must have been covered one time by sergeant's stripes. Nobody ever asked him why he'd been busted. It could have been one thing or another, it didn't seem to matter. They all knew he was going down. He drank wine, regularly. His small face was purple and warped, and tiny red veins were like scratches on his cheekbones. He sat with eyes like soft brown marbles. Later, when it would be dark, he would go into the meadow and buy wine from the Frenchmen. Sometimes in the late evening he would stumble back into the hut, his cheeks fired with the straining light of drunken communion. But now as they talked of Callan he stared at the stove, watching the pulsating cherry-red color, a color that moved at its belly, bloating bright red, then sucking back to a deep maroon, constant and regular, like breathing. His fuzzy old hands were nervous on his thighs.

Of the men in the hut, Tom Swanson probably liked the Negro best. He had watched him working in the gas depot, a good worker, the type of man who went ahead quietly while the others complained. He had no pretense about him. When he talked of the sergeant, it was groping, slow, like an attempt to understand.

"I only got five months lef' over here," he said. "I'm just gonna do my work an Saturday night I'm gonna drink that good vin blanc. I'm not gonna do nothin extrawdnary. No sir. That man, he's the kine that watches an waits, an when he gets the chance, boom, you is in jail the rest a you life. Yes sir He's the kine a man who has to be doin somethin an I don't want him doin nothin to old Aldous."

"Why're you staying in nights, Tom?" asked Sam suddenly. "I never seen you stay in a week running before. Huh?"

"Just taking it easy." He had not spoken most of the night. The sound of his own voice startled him.

"Yeah? The other night you go outa here all dressed in them French clothes an five minutes later you're back undressing for bed. Huh?" He seemed happy with this perception, pushing ahead where he would have remained silent if they were alone. "Girl stand you up?"

Sam's leering face annoyed him. "Hell, I came back because I missed you. Missed the sight of that nice soft butt." He was a little relieved when the man snorted and turned away. He didn't like the vehemence in his humor nor did he like to use it as a defense.

That night, when he had come back to the hut after preparing to see Solange, he had tried to be amused with himself. All day he had been thinking of her, thinking of going on pass. First he had shaved and showered, then waited until he was sure Callan would be gone from the Orderly room. He didn't even consider why he was waiting. Then he had gone in and taken down the overnight ledger. He signed his name on the blank page for that date and the signature, alone, possessed a strange vividness. He would be the only man taking a pass. Callan would look at his name there alone. With a peculiar heat at his temples he erased his name and went back to the hut.

Afterward, he'd been disgusted. He knew there had been no reason to do that. He had lain on his bunk and done his best to be amused with himself.

Aldous Brown interrupted the reflection. "What do you think of Callan?" he said. It startled him. He could feel himself fluster as their attention focused.

"I don't know."

There was a curious quiet, a waiting. "What d'yuh mean, you like him?" accused Sam.

"I haven't even thought about it," he said casually, and inside he was red. "You probably think too much about it." He looked around at the men in the room. He looked at Aldous Brown. He knew the Negro liked him, admired him even. There was always that respect in his voice. "Dammit, don't ask me. I don't know him better than any of you."

Aldous Brown watched him curiously. "What's, he got you bugged or somethin?"

Swanson had never heard the word, but he understood it at once, like a code that could only be caught by a particular susceptibility. Aldous Brown watched him, interested, not unkind.

"What do you mean, bugged?"

The Negro shrugged his shoulders, as if he did not know himself.

"You oughta know he's a bastard," said Sam. "The way he jumped on you the first day at formation. He didn't have no right to do that."

Swanson put his boots down on the floor carefully, side by side, giving himself time. "I don't know what to think." In the room there was a pause, as if the air were a problem, thick as a substance.

"Well, he better not fool with me," muttered Sam.

Chapter Seven

As he worked during the days his mind was full of
the girl. He could see her blondness, the almost
white hair, or think of the clean smell of her. It
gave him a surge of lightness. One week end he
would take her to the park, down by the stream
with its banks of planted lawn. He had put his
hand in that stream once and felt its coolness, not
lazy water as in other parks, but a good mountain
coolness. He wanted to take her there.

But why was he thinking of the future when a
week of evenings had already passed? He wanted
to go to Bordeaux and he wanted to see Solange.
It was simple, he told himself. As he worked he
ridiculed the sudden timidness or that in himself
which had prevented him from leaving the camp.

After formation that night he dressed and went
directly to the Orderly shack. Callan was alone at
the far desk and he entered and went to the sign-
out ledger without looking toward him. He signed
it hurriedly. But when he laid down the pencil
there was a sensation of emptiness, a moment in

time. He could hear the hum of the electric light in the ceiling.

"All right, Swanson."

He turned quickly. "What!"

The sergeant stared. "What?" he repeated, a curious roll to the word. He stared and chuckled, as if he were secure in an advantage. "You been thinking about the job, Swanson?"

"Yes." It was someone else's answer, not his own. He had not let himself think of the job.

"Well?"

"I wish . . . I wish you could give me a little more time."

The sergeant continued to stare. He leaned back in the chair, smiling. "Sure," he said. "You take all the time you need."

He went down the road with none of the old good feeling. As he drew farther from the camp he could sense it behind him, physically, like someone's finger near the small of his back. He went on without turning to hitch-hike. At the crossroads to Bordeaux he continued straight ahead, along another dirt road that led to a little-known village. He fixed that in his mind as his destination, his purpose. He tried to think only of that, of walking until he reached this village. It was cold, with a thinness of fog hanging just above the vineyards. His feet scuffled over the road and he could feel the cold in them, the pain. He began to count each step, one two three four, the intervals between counts seeming treacherously long.

At the village he went into the only bar, ordering cognac from the proprietor, who sat alone reading a paper. "Have you got a telephone?" he asked in French.

The proprietor regarded him. "For where?"

"Bordeaux."

"Hundred francs for Bordeaux."

He laid out the bill and went to the rear where the man pointed. It was several minutes before the call went through and when he heard her voice it was close, startling, yet at the same time distant as from another world. "Solange?"

"Yes."

"It's me, Tom."

"Tom! Where are you?"

"Out near the camp. I called to ask if I could see you this week end."

"Well . . ." Her voice hesitated. "Certainly. But I've been thinking of you during the week."

He glanced over the bare kitchen in which the phone was located. He had the cognac with him and he pushed down an impulse to drink from it.

"I was going to come in tonight," he said. Then he listened to his own silence. He couldn't finish it. He was almost sick in the long silence.

"Is anything wrong?" came her voice.

"No," he said finally. "Look, Solange, I'll see you Saturday afternoon in the park, about two o'clock near the benches."

When he hung up the phone he went back to the bar and asked for another cognac. He stayed until he knew he was drunk. Once the proprietor

looked up from his newspaper and asked him if he
didn't think the weather was becoming cold. Swanson lit a cigarette instead of answering and went
on with his drinking.

Saturday was three days off. One night he came
out of the hut and walked to the edge of the
meadow. The night was hard, blue-black. Across
the meadow a small orange fire flickered. He stood
for a while alone. Off to the right drifted laughter
from the enlisted men's club.

He thought of his parents. It had been several
weeks since he'd written them and he speculated
about going back to the hut and starting a letter.
Somehow, he was reluctant to think of his parents.
He walked toward the enlisted men's club, where
he'd been several times lately.

The outside patio was empty and he ordered a
beer through the window counter, then set upright
an overturned patio chair. He sat alone in the dark,
thinking of Sergeant Callan, a picture of the man's
face, tough-skinned, close and confident as in the
Orderly room. A picture of him moving, walking.
In the dark he experienced a little spasm of the
sense, a vague passing through. He tried to concen-
trate on the flicker of the distant orange fire.

"Swanson."

He tightened in his chair, for it was his voice,
Callan's, a whisper from the night.

He appeared slowly from the darkness. He had a
can of beer in his hand, his face pale, round like
the moon as it stared from above. "Why were you

frightened," he said, but it was not a question. He reached for a chair and sat down opposite, smiling, the face darker, more living in its closeness. "I frightened you, didn't I?" He said it curious, gloating. "I drink out here too. I've watched you before."

"I was thinking when you called my name. It startled me."

"What were you thinking of."

"Nothing. Nothing much."

Sergeant Callan took a long drink from his can. He set it on the ground, staring at the boy. "You coming to work for me?"

The question hung in the night, like the expected beat of a drum, straining, sounding, then rolling soft through the air. He was enveloped, trapped, caught in a rhythm outside himself. "No." It was an effort, a whisper. He didn't know if he'd spoken or not.

"You're coming to work for me aren't you?"

"All right," he said softly.

The sergeant leaned back in his chair. He picked up the empty beer can from the ground and rolled it slowly between his palms. "Sure you are. I knew you would."

Chapter Eight

On Saturday, he left for Bordeaux with two days of the Orderly room behind him. He hurried down the road toward the highway, wanting to feel himself drawing away from the camp, wanting to feel his own long strides and the current they ran through his body.

The tenseness of the two days, their reality, spurred him on. Now he knew how bad it was and the knowing did not make him easier. The work itself he disliked, the typing, the filing, the endless detail involved in memorandum, rosters, company orders; it was the kind of work that pricked against the senses. But worse was Callan's presence, ten feet across, speaking only rarely and then to give instructions in a voice that was cold and harsh. The man never seemed to be absorbed in what he was doing; even when he was bent over his paper work, there was that sense of his being conscious of more, watching.

For the first time Swanson could think of it without its closeness. He was alone, walking, a sunny day, and he was a little proud to know he could think of it without the pull, the depression. With Solange he was going to talk about it from beginning to end. She would understand anything, that girl. God, she was the one. A college girl but like none he'd known before. The things she said, they seemed to spring out real and true, all her own, nothing rehearsed.

She'd never asked him much about himself, nothing about his age or education, about what his father did for a living. It was because of something good in her, he knew that now. Once he feared it might be a lack of interest, but now, right now, he knew differently. It was a quality, her not having to ask about him, a thing she had developed that allowed her to wait and let everything come out natural in their being together. It was rare. Her patience was like a compliment, a sign of trust.

I want her to know me, he thought. Everything. Completely. I want to lie down in that soft grass at the park and talk to her, just let it come.

The thought of it made him feel safe.

The banks of the little creek were planted in lawn, soft as a green towel. In several places wooden bridges arched over, and on the closest of these a young Frenchman and his girl leaned from the rail, dropping bread hunks for the perch. He watched them.

There were few people in the park, no other soldiers, and he was suddenly pleased with his clothes, the French pants and coat. He was an infiltrator, a happy impostor. Perhaps the couple would pass by his bench when they left the bridge. He'd salute them. "Bonjour, il fait beau, n'est-ce pas?" Casually in the sun, lazily done, one Frenchman to another.

He leaned back on the warmth of the bench and smiled. A viewer of mankind, he was. A transient with royal blood. Ah, a great oaf upon a park bench!

He saw Solange coming over the little bridge.

She came directly toward him, all the beauty of her, and as she drew near he was almost frightened, excited with a nervous joy. She walked up to within a foot of him.

"You're beautiful," he exclaimed.

She laughed with delight and shook his hand, not so much a greeting as a culmination, a capping of the few seconds.

"You make me feel beautiful inside," he said. It was true and like nothing he had ever said before. He felt he could say anything and it would be right.

"You're so happy today!"

He laughed into the air and reached out to put an arm around her. His hand was on her waist where the stuff of her sweater was dry and glowing. "I'm happy, sure. I'm exploding."

"And are you crazy too?"

"Crazy? Sure I'm crazy!"

With his arm around her waist she was standing almost against him, the head tilted back, her eyes with a playful wariness. "Now is it me that makes you this way, or getting away from that camp?"

"Definitely you. Just a little getting away from camp."

"Oh, you're miserable. Terrible!"

"I'm the most miserable man alive."

"You are. You're worse than the most miserable man alive."

"I should commit suicide."

"I doubt that you would. I dare you."

Together they ran down to the bank of the creek. He held her hand and peered into the swift water and then he frowned. "Later, tomorrow maybe," he said.

"Ah-ha!"

"It's such a beautiful day, sunny, warm, blue. Why should I do it on a day like this?"

She leaned in close to him, her nose and mouth warm against the hollow of his neck. For a moment they stood like that, but then she pulled away. It was not coquettish, her pulling away, she was smiling still. He'd noticed it before, that restraint, as if she were refusing to take advantage of his exuberance.

Together, they sat on the green bank of the stream.

"You know, I never think of you as a soldier. I'm thinking of you always as just a young man who comes in from the country at night. Is that silly? On week ends I see the soldiers in their uniforms and they're not like you. You seem alone, separate."

Somehow it pleased him. Not vainly, but it pleased him because it sparked an undercurrent of feeling. "You know, I think about that," he said. "Have you ever watched them in the streets? The soldiers? Listen," he urged lightly. "They're two kinds that come into town on week ends, Saturday soldiers and Sunday soldiers. The Saturdays you can tell in a minute. If they look like they don't give a damn, then they're Saturdays. They get off the bus around noon, walk around not giving a damn, drink a little in the bars around Place Gambetta, and by dark they're good and drunk so they buy themselves a girl, take her to a hotel room, boom bam thankyou ma'am, and then they come down and meet the midnight bus back to camp. . . . It's all right, this talk, isn't it?"

She nodded.

"Now, Sunday soldiers come in on Sunday, naturally. A very different type. There they are, clustered in the street, three or four together, two years of college for each of them, faces scrubbed clean and cameras strapped like rifles to their shoulders." Like an actor, he stood up to illustrate. "Always, they're starting to go somewhere, going to snap a photo somewhere or see something new and exciting. So all day they wander like kids lost at a carnival. But at seven o'clock they assemble. At seven, promptly, they can be observed having quiet little dinners in those quaint restaurants near the fish market. And I promise you, each of them has a certain light on his face, a light that says they're very aware that they're having dinner in a quaint little restaurant in the bohemian district of Bordeaux, France."

With the description finished he made a half-bow which Solange received with a steady patter of applause.

"Bravo. Quite good. And you, where do you fit in this eloquent picture?"

"Ah, there you have me. I am the man of mystery, the undefinable."

"You are the wonderful," she said.

Smiling, he sat again beside her. "I don't mean all of that. Not so much, anyhow."

"It's probably just how it is." Her hand picked at the grass and then her blue eyes were rather serious. "Is it bad at the camp?"

The question was sobering, yet it did not cool him. As earlier on the road, he felt the inclination to talk with her. "Sometimes it is bad," he admitted. "It's bad, yet it doesn't have to be. A lot of the men make it bad for themselves. The camp is kind of a habit they get into and then they lose their spirit."

"But you've never gotten into that habit. You're always here in Bordeaux, you've learned French. . . ." She paused. "You're full of life," she said.

He sloughed it off. "I'm just full of beans."

"No," she persisted gently, "you're full of life. Even that first day when we met at the café, I could see it then. You have a real feeling for living." She

touched his arm with a little laugh. "Don't be embarrassed. It's true, you know. Oh, it's not an intel-
lectual thing, maybe that's why it embarrasses
you. But you're perceptive and it comes out in so
many ways, in your reaction to things. That's why
I ask about the camp. With a feeling person I
should think it would be even more of an ordeal.
And yet you're not depressed by it, you're happy
and you've got your spirit, your zest. To me that
seems wonderful. You have the openness and a spe-
cial kind of strength to match it."

It stimulated him, cleanly, hearing her say that.
The first embarrassment dissolved and he found
himself considering her words, looking at himself
along with her.

Maybe it was true that he felt the sordidness,
the whole environment more than the others. He
could be in the hut listening to idle talk and its
idleness would be suddenly as vivid as a revelation
and his ears would burn as if he were alone in his
listening. Or to watch the men, anywhere—in the
recreation room, at pool—to see their attitudes so
fixed even when they were relaxing. Tired, old.
Like men in a picture, some artist's conception of
the grayness of the camp. Yet it wasn't that he was
really watching or hearing. He wasn't standing
back. He was there, in it, in it with the heat of his
chest. Deeply, he could know the men around him.
It didn't take words. Their nearness seemed
enough, stronger than some voice shouting happiness! pain! Their nearness was like a finger moving
within, like a shadow as it speared across the

orange ground of a fire. Was that foolish? Was it awareness? Perception?

Sometimes he wanted to cry out to the people around him. Do you feel this like I do? Can't you see it? And the urge to cry out was not to show or tell them anything. He wanted to know, truly, wanted to know if they felt and saw it as strongly as he.

Once he had tried to speak to Sam about the joy of hitch-hiking the road to Bordeaux. But it was almost in ridicule that Sam had responded. Perhaps it had been in the way he tried to tell it, for he'd seen that same blank response on the faces of townspeople at home, times when he was full, exuberant, talking of things that had moved him. "Now, Tom," they answered, and through knowing him they were good-natured—"Now Tom, fifteen or twenty years I been around them hills you speak of, and I sure ain't seen 'em purple colored or smelled any 'mountain odor.'"

He had taken even to ridiculing himself.

But Solange . . . When he spoke, she knew what he meant. And it wasn't that she was being kind or pretending. He could actually see the response well up inside her, come up to her face and make it even more alive. Don't be embarrassed, she'd told him, or don't be afraid, perhaps she meant. As if it were a thing to be proud of.

He was happy, grateful that she was there, grateful that he'd been allowed to know her at all. He turned so that he was close to her. "Dammit," he said happily.

"See! Your most endearing term and it's dammit."

"I guess that's just the way I am."

"And I bet it's not just the way you are."

He was grinning and it was the kind of grin that warmed him clear through. He kissed her lips and let himself go to the nearness of her. Their bodies touched as they lay on the bank of the stream. He kissed her, and when he raised his head he saw the pink neck and then the grass and then the stream and the little bridge with the young couple still there, the man's arm around the girl.

"It's so good," she murmured. "It's so good to be here with you."

He lay back on the lawn into the laziness of the sky above, his legs and arms alive and intensely peaceful. He let his eyes close and felt the gentleness of the sun on his skin. Her hand was on his chest and she was watching him.

"You can relax so well," she said presently. "Is it because you like to work? You do like work, don't you?"

"I do." He opened his eyes but did not move. "You know, out at the camp I'm a laborer, a kind of flunky in the gas depot, but it's good anyhow. It's gotten so I hardly think of time passing or what I'm doing, and yet I think strongly about what I'm doing. But I'm not watching myself, do you know? All we do is stack barrels, hoist them, stack them, hoist them, stack them. But when you get into it, it's a clean feeling, and when the day's over you're sharp and ready to be free."

He only partly realized that he was describing a job he no longer had. As he spoke it seemed true, happy, poetic nearly, and nothing else seemed to matter. "My father is the same way about his work. He's been a plumber for twenty-five years. Once I think I was ashamed of my father being a plumber, but now I'm ashamed for having been ashamed." He looked up at her. "For him, it isn't so much the kind of work as the spirit of it. I've never actually talked to him about it, but it's the kind of thing you don't have to talk about to know. I'm sure he feels that way. He takes a real pleasure in things. And my mother, she's the same way. She's taken care of him and us kids, cooks, does the housework, and I think she does it all because mostly she enjoys it."

"How many are in your family?"

"Well, I've got an older sister and an older brother. Ellie got married about a year ago to a lawyer there in town and my brother is in his last year at college. The folks are always saying that we kids have turned out twice as good as themselves, but it's just something they say. They're happy with themselves and they're happy with us and that's all there is to it. Does it sound like I'm making it all too good?"

"No, it doesn't," she said. "It sounds like you're telling just how it is. Are you going to go back there when you finish with the Army?"

"I don't know what I'll do. I guess you're asking what I'm going to do for a living, and honestly, I don't know. I'll be going to college first so there'll be more time to decide. Maybe I should be more concerned or ambitious but I just figure it will all come."

"I think it will too. And people who get too concerned over that kind of thing make me nervous."

He laughed and sat up. Sitting up was a bit like coming into reality. He blinked the sun out of his eyes. The young couple had left the bridge and he saw them walking down the path directly behind them. He turned quickly and made a short wave. "Bonjour," he called, "il fait beau, n'est-ce pas?"

"Bonjour," they both returned, smiling, and as they passed by the Frenchman leaned close, hugging his girl's waist.

Chapter Nine

In front of the terrace afternoon shadows speared across the pavement and pedestrians swarmed over them without glancing down. The Avenue de Tourneau flashed heavily with week-end traffic. Occasionally an American Army truck would rumble by and less often a soldier would pass with the sidewalk crowd. "They never come to this part of town," he told her, and then they looked up to see a soldier lurch off the sidewalk and lean drunkenly on the terrace wall. It was startling. The soldier moved his head from side to side, fixing his gaze with an effort upon the people drinking above him. Swanson saw at once that it was Cowley. "That fellow's in my outfit," he said sharply.

Cowley's gaze skittered past then returned and focused, blooming into recognition. "Swanson!"

He stumbled down the length of the wall and stepped onto the terrace, weaving toward them in a dedicated way while curious faces turned to watch his progress. "Ol' Swans!" he chanted, throwing an arm around Tom's neck. The boy disengaged himself by standing up.

"Hello, Cowley. Here, sit down."

Cowley plopped himself into a chair, his elbow tipping an empty glass.

"Solange, this is Cowley from my company."

"First name's George," he muttered. "Plenty drunk, Swans." He spoke down at the table top. "Drunker'n hell. Gonna go d'bed. First I'm gonna get me a piece of ass an then I'm gonna go d'bed."

Tom looked at Solange and her face was calm. There's nothing to do, he thought. He's drunk. A drunk like this wouldn't upset her. And yet it suddenly seemed more serious. He hadn't spoken of Callan or the clerk's job and now there was this appearance of Cowley. Why hadn't he told her? It was what he had wanted to speak of right from the beginning. What good was all that other talk now?

His skin was heated, prickling. What would this guy say? The bastard. It was easy to see why Callan had fired him. Weak, whining, the kind of personality that would grind anyone.

"Goddamn. Swanson, ol' Swans," blubbered Cowley, reaching out to grab his sleeve. "Let's have a beer, three of 'em. C'mon, I'm buyin." His hand flopped at the waiter. "Twa beers," he shouted, holding tight to the sleeve. "Ol' Swanson, ol' company clerk." He peered intently at Tom, his eyes making a sudden accusation. "Think you're a big shot now, dontcha?"

"No. Not at all." Even in his anger he was dis-

gusted with the sound of "not at all." "Come on,
relax, Cowley."

"Relax? Humph! Shit! It's you who's gonna hafta
relax. Yuh think you're a big shot now, just go
ahead and think it. Go on. You'll find out."

Swanson tried to get himself quiet. He could feel
Solange watching him. "Where do you work now?"

"Where d'yuh think? In the field." His head
stooped over the beer. His lower lip hung out from
the pyramid of pimples and he seemed suddenly
helpless, subdued. "You'll see. That guy is a sonofabitch. He'll fix you, some way. You wait," he
whimpered, and he looked at them both, heavily,
as if to have them know the seriousness of what he
said. But then his chin dropped toward his chest
and he whimpered again. The muscles of his neck
were exposed, very red and straining, and then
they eased and his head hung quietly.

Swanson knew they should get up and leave, yet
he sat staring past Cowley out to the sidewalk
crowds. He couldn't bring himself to turn toward
Solange. How would it be now with her? Would
she be thinking him some kind of a fraud? Over a
small thing like this? That's it. It was a little thing
and why should he be so upset? If he hadn't told
her about the job, all right, so what, what was
wrong with that?

His thoughts came like the red prickle of excitement, but through it all there was a real and bitter
disappointment. It wasn't a little thing and there
was something very wrong and he knew if he tried
to make it otherwise it would be worse. He looked

again at Cowley, at the circle of misery that was almost palpable around him. He knew that none of it was Cowley's fault. It had nothing to do with him.

"Let's go," he said. He left a bill for the drinks and they went down from the terrace, Solange stepping rapidly beside him. There was a throbbing in his arms and chest, a throbbing as real as tears. Had there been a death? A father? A mother? He felt blurred over with loss, blind in the streets. The crowds swept by like yelling ghosts and there she was beside him, the only thing, there were her footsteps, walking, waiting.

He took her arm and they moved against a building.

"Look, that fellow was the old clerk in my company. I'm the new clerk. I didn't tell you I had a new job. They just gave it to me the other day and I was going to tell you about it in the park. It's not so important anyhow. Hell, it's not important."

The center points of her blue eyes were on him, curious, concerned.

"Cowley figures he got a bad deal, I guess. Maybe he did, I don't know. I didn't want the damn job in the first place, it was like being forced into it. Maybe that's not right either, Jesus, I don't know. I'm working for this Callan, he's a master sergeant, the first sergeant. He's not as bad as they think, really, he's not like they say. They don't say anything, I mean they just think of him as a tough character. Actually, I don't like him myself. I'm not defending him, understand. Dammit!"

His head shook in helpless anger. She watched him without speaking and then her hand reached out and was tentative on his arm. "All right," she said softly, and at that moment as he looked at her he was filled with gratefulness, a feeling that flooded through him and as quickly washed away, leaving him empty against the building, empty with a core of nervousness. With a movement that was almost involuntary, he took his arm away from her hand.

"Where would you like to go?"

"Anywhere you'd like."

"We should go somewhere," he said.

They began walking again until they reached an intersection. It marked one corner of a large square, the Place Gambetta, and at the opposite end were the little side streets where the soldiers' bars were jammed as on a boardwalk. "You ever been in one of those bars?"

She shook her head. "Is that where the Saturday soldiers go?"

He stood on the edge of the curb without answering.

"Did you want to take me there?"

He shrugged his shoulders and vacantly watched the traffic.

"You're speaking of the bars across the Place Gambetta?" she questioned, pronouncing "Gambetta" in the true French, a word the soldiers uttered harshly with a leer, and now the sweetness

of its sound was startling in its innocence, and as
he stood on the curb the empty feeling seemed to
grow and expand.

"I've never been there," she said. "But I'll go,
certainly I'll go if you like."

He stared at the distant curb, a gray and undu-
lating cliff from another world. "All right, c'mon."

They passed through the traffic and crossed the
square, going down the nearest of the side streets.
Immediately there was a change in color, a darkness made by the close, overhanging buildings. The
air seemed thin and still, and the surface of the
street was a thousand little domes of cobblestones.
Farther down where the first bars began it was
lighter. The endless neon blinked pale and weird
in the afternoon, the glow reflecting a faint dust
that filtered from the old upper buildings, steady,
as soft as sorrow.

Soldiers passed them on the street. Alone, they
passed with bent heads, and when they came in
groups they leered openly at Solange. He stared
back defiantly, ashamed already, yet guiding her
on. "Are you afraid?"

"Afraid? No, I'm not afraid."

But he couldn't tell what she was thinking. She
seemed a stranger beside him, superior.

"Are we going in one?" she asked.

"We might as well, we've come this far." He
spoke as if to touch her and fill the emptiness.

The bars were nestled into the bottom stories of
the buildings, their fronts painted red or yellow,
and soldiers clustered around the doorways, hang-

ing on the lip of the inside frenzy. He followed close behind her as they turned in and shouldered through a group of suddenly quiet soldiers, who with drunken deliberateness made a little pathway for them. When they had passed he could hear them burst into laughter.

Inside, the bar was lined with enlisted men, a woman wedged between every three or four. Men stood stupid drunk in the aisle between the bar and tables, and at the tables they leaned away from their drinks and shouted to friends at the bar, arms shooting out to grab at women who pushed business-like and laughing through the throng. Solange sat down quickly at a small table near the entrance and he found a loose chair and pulled it up beside her. In the heated atmosphere it was even darker, a pulsing heaviness strange to the afternoon outside.

An older woman who was apparently the proprietress, a full-breasted, pock-marked woman, poured rapid little glasses of cognac, sweeping francs from the zinc bar into a trough behind, while her helper, a girl of twelve or thirteen, moved like a bird among the bottles and glasses, bending often for fresh bottles, her backside exposed and jabbed by men leaning far over the bar. Each time, she found her bottle and went impassively, swiftly about her business, while around her the air was bloated with voices, pushed tight like air in a balloon, strained against the poster-covered walls.

They saw a soldier at a nearby table labor to his

feet, the cognac sloshing from his glass onto the belly of his uniform. "That's my woman!" he challenged, pointing at a girl with creviced breasts who straddled the knee of a man at another table. "You hear me, she's my woman!"

"What d'yuh mean, she's your woman?" answered the other, the motion of his knee covered by the girl's dress.

"I mean that's my woman."

"Yours and forty other guys'."

"Listen, sonofabitch," and his voice heightened beyond the noise of the room. "She and me is goin upstairs together."

The girl perked up, sat straighter on the swinging knee.

"So that makes her your woman! Well let me tell you, buddy, I been countin. You go upstairs with her and you'll be number eight. Number eight today, buddy!"

The first soldier grinned, drunk, suddenly amiable. "Number eight, shit. I'm gonna be number eight, nine, ten."

The girl, evidently sensing a more serious admirer, began to struggle away from the soldier's knee. She made a little squeal of practiced protest. "Let go, son-bitch. You no touch me. You pay mille franc for touch me."

"I'll touch you if I want, baby."

"You son-bitch. You think you hansome? You pay mille franc for touch me." The girl struggled free, shook herself disdainfully, then cuddled against the standing man.

"Eight, nine, ten, honey. That's me."

"Shure. You nice. You got mille franc, honey?"

"Damn rights I got mille franc. I'm old eight nine ten, ain't I?" The two of them, arms entwined, bumped through the crowd toward the back stairs.

"Buy me a cognac, Fred," complained the man left behind. He slapped at the shoulder of the soldier next to him. "Goddamn, Fred, buy me a cognac." Fred's head lolled unanswering. Once more he slapped at him, pushed at his shoulder, and Fred teetered and slumped from the chair onto the floor and he sat there an instant and then collapsed between the chair legs.

"Goddamn!" The soldier's eyes swept past them, covering the entire room with his plea. "Gimme a cognac, somebody! Hey, goddamn sonofabitch Madame what's your name, I wanna cognac, hear!"

Swanson had seen it all before. I've seen it a dozen times, he thought quickly. And I've seen it plenty of times when I thought it was funny. But now it held a certain horror. His body felt cold, separate, and he was conscious only of the girl beside him, conscious of her expressionless face and the thin line of a mouth.

"In a way it's funny," he tried.

"Perhaps it is," she answered after a moment. She stared at a vacant spot in the mass of activity. "It's just that in a place like this I feel I'm watching. I hate that feeling."

His ears were burning with shame and yet he continued to sit. "Do you want something to drink?"

"No. You take something, though."

He sat for a moment longer. Soldiers were beginning to turn in their direction, their glances
rolling down her blond figure. Let one of them
make a crack, he thought. Let one of them come
around this table. It was almost a wish, desperate,
and beneath the table there was a lightness to his
clenched fists that was dreamlike. If they could
touch against a cheekbone, crush against one! Anybody! He wanted to fight or shout and he lowered
his head as if to stifle a cry. Then he took her hand
and pulled her quickly to her feet. "C'mon, let's
go!"

Without speaking they pushed out through the
bunched doorway and moved rapidly up the dark
street. He didn't release her hand or slow until
they had come out on the square.

"I swear, Solange. I don't know what's wrong
with me."

"Don't. It doesn't matter. Let's go back to the
park and walk for a while."

"No. Listen, I swear, I feel rotten. I don't know
what's wrong with me."

She hesitated, seeming to realize it was not an
apology he was trying to make. His hand pulled
down over the tenseness of his jaw. "I just don't
know."

"What is it, Tom?"

He shook his head. "Look," he faced her suddenly, "I think I'd better go."

"Go?"

"I think I'd better."

She stared at him. "All right, if that's what you want."

"I'll walk you home."

"No," she said quickly. "You can leave me here. Please, you go on, I can do some shopping."

He could see the strain on her face. He turned from her helplessly. I'll see you soon," he blurted, and he began walking through the crowd with her strained, hurt face vivid in front of him. He walked with a crazy sense of his own velocity, half blind, swinging by instinct to avoid collisions. The walls of buildings swooped by and he thought, Can I choke a building? Has a building got a throat to take hold of? There were tears in the hollow of his belly and the emptiness was boiling full, with shame, with anger, what was it? That girl. Why had he treated her like that, that good girl, the best girl he'd ever met, the girl he wanted to be so careful with, just at first, careful so that she would know him and then he could have been anything because she would have known him and it would have been right, and now he felt unclean and no damn good. Why should she want to know him when he was like this? It was all broken and tattered and empty. Cowley, it was that goddamned Cowley, it had started then. But it wasn't him, no, don't blame it on Cowley. And don't blame it on the bar. It's me, he thought, it's me. Twenty years old, just beginning to look around and think I'm fine and now feeling like this, like everything's gone for nothing and I'm no more than this no-damn-goodness right now.

He knew that he could actually cry, that tears would be coming from his eyes and down his cheeks. Twenty years old and crying, he thought wildly. A man, Christ no goddamned man at all— a boy, a baby, a punk. That bastard, that rotten dirty bastard. He'd kill him, that Callan, take him with bare hands on the throat.

Until dark he was in the streets, past the brightness of stores and cafés, along the gray of the waterfront, and after dark he sat alone in a bar and drank cognac until he was so drunk he could hardly feel the patron lift him into the street before closing.

Chapter Ten

It rained in the next weeks. It rained in the nights, a mixture of wet and wind that hollowed out the huts and swept away the heat from the stoves. The men curled cocoon-like beneath their blankets. It rained during the days, not windy then, but steady, pallid warm drops out of the white haze above. Muddy streams guttered the wooden sidewalks. The wet glistened dull on the gravel streets.

The Orderly room was better built than the huts. In the daytime it warmed against the weather, the air inside still, without motion. Swanson spent them at his desk, the sergeant opposite him. They rarely spoke. The sergeant did not often glance up from his work. There was a heavy silence between them.

One evening, standing in a slicker before the formation, he told them there would be no more passes until the rains ended. The roads were slick and filmed with mud and it seemed a reasonable order, but as he spoke his eyes were rapid and **ex-**

cited. "Is it clear?" pierced his voice through the rain. It had a sharpness close to exhilaration. "Is it clear when I say you're restricted? I mean all of you!"

Callan seemed to like the weather. Often he would get up from the desk and stand outside the door under the eave of the roof, sniffing the wetness, the white damp air. It seemed to bring him a comfort, tightening the world of the camp, bringing it closer and workable around him. In the mornings he did his paper work steadily, without hurry, his ruddy face relaxed, as if there were a cushion now, a pause. When company business brought men into the office he listened to them easily, his arms folded on the desk. He appeared to consider their routine problems with the same seriousness in which they were delivered. He returned their talk quietly. Sometimes his mouth would crook in a smile, a flash of good humor.

But with Swanson he never showed a looseness. When there was something to be said he spoke directly, hard, with a riveted gaze. Other times when his eyes fell absently on the boy he would shift them quickly away.

The restriction on passes did not affect Swanson. Bordeaux and the thought of Solange had become thickly entwined, and he'd resolved not to see her until he felt differently. What he wanted was the moment when he could sound himself to the sergeant. He wanted to cut through the leaden throb of the office. He wanted to cut into the man himself.

And once the sergeant asked him, "How do you like your work?" It was a question that came sharply in the midst of a long silence. And though he had waited for such a question there was only the rise of his blood, and his mind fogged over until his reply came muffled like a child's. "It's all right."

But the sergeant had a curious knowing look about him, almost pleased. "You'd better. You're stuck, so you'd better like it."

There were times though when he actually appeared to struggle toward a kindness, a looseness with the boy. He tried occasionally to compliment him. Rising from the desk he would face away toward the window, his full back tight beneath the khaki shirt. His whole body pondered with the effort. "You're doing a good job," he might say, his back stiff, facing away.

After three days of rain a telephone call came from the captain in Bordeaux. Swanson could hear the distinct, metallic-sounding voice as it spoke to Callan.

"Listen, can you get along without me today? God, sergeant, the rain is something fierce in here. I doubt if my car can make it, you know what the rain does to these French roads. You can make it all right without me? Ah, that's good, that's fine. Listen, I might be stuck tomorrow too, maybe a couple of days. Smooth things over will you, you know, if any brass come in."

As the sergeant set down the phone he turned to Swanson and his face was unprepared. It was boy-

ish and eager. "Well I guess we can do all right
without him, don't you think? You bet!" He
walked about the room chuckling, his fists
clenched in excitement. He walked to Swanson's
desk. "What do you think, huh!" He slapped him
on the shoulder. "Ol' Swanson and I can run the
company, you bet!"

It seemed shameful, his sudden happiness. Swanson moved his shoulder and forced down an impulse toward pity. He stared coldly at the sergeant.
And Callan, as if he'd suddenly glimpsed himself,
turned blank and frowned. His lips tightened and
he turned and left the office, grim, patting his
thighs.

It was later that same day when the sergeant
appeared in the recreation room. He had never
been there before, and the room quieted when he
came in. In the trail of talk there was only the
lonesome and separate crack of a cue ball. He stood
back off from the players, alone, a boyish half-
smile on his face. After the first silence the men
at the table went on with their game. The room
was crowded and smoky and the talk did not return to normal. The players moved self-consciously
around the table and the onlookers shuffled resentfully in the background. He stood alone, hands
shy in his pockets, the thumbs lapping over.

The men began to steal quick glances in his direction. It was almost awe they felt, having him
close in a social atmosphere. One after another
they turned secretly and glimpsed him standing
there.

As they watched him half smiling, asking nothing, some of them dropped their eyes to the floor, as if they were embarrassed. There was something about his isolated figure that caused a tinge of pity, not disrespect, but a gentle pity.

When the game ended, the man in line for the next turn took the cue stick, then hesitated. He offered it to the sergeant. "Take a try, Sergeant Callan."

He accepted the cue stick with a surprised smile. And as he set himself to break the triangle the men watched with a strange eagerness. It was a mediocre shot that he made, and through the rest of the game his playing was rather poor and fumbling. Occasionally he would comment on his playing or make a common pool joke. The men laughed, almost anxiously.

When he'd finished he passed on the stick and stepped back from the table. He stood for a while longer, his hands placed childlike in his pockets. He turned to go and before he had reached the door several of the soldiers had spoken out to him.

"So long, Sergeant."

"See you, Sergeant."

When he had gone the atmosphere did not return to its previous lightness. They continued playing, but in a careless way, as though their thoughts were elsewhere.

"He can be all right when he wants to be," offered one of them.

They seemed to mull it over in the new quiet.

"He ain't such a bad guy," said another.

But that night and the next the sergeant kept Swanson in the Orderly room. "This isn't the kind of job where you drop everything at five and leave," he said. "You're going to have to expect this now and then."

But he was given work that easily could have been done during the day, and he went ahead with it and forced himself to think of nothing. He knew not to complain. In the full air of the little room, a complaint would spring up vivid like a cry.

Callan sat across at the other desk, shuffling through duty rosters that Swanson knew had been finished the week before. Often he would lay them aside and stare at the wall, as if it were an excuse to remain, as if it were absorbing.

On the second evening the rain had quieted some. It fell lightly on the tar-papered roof and rolled like a film down the panes of the window. The stove worked in its steady, breathing way. Then they both looked up as they heard a scratching noise from the rear of the shack. It came unique and separate from the patter of rain, sounding again, a sharpness running across the boards. The sergeant got up from his desk and Swanson jumped up and followed him to the rear of the shack.

It was the old man from his hut, Pop Henneken, lying in the weeds by the warmth of the wall, his purple-coated mouth ajar in drunken sleep. Swanson felt himself quiver, once, and he looked quickly at Callan. The sergeant stared down as though hypnotized. He stared down and his foot seemed to inch toward the old man's belly. "I can court-martial him for this," he said softly.

"Don't do it, please."

He looked blank at Swanson and returned his gaze to the curled figure in the weeds. "I can bust him. I can do more than that. I've watched him before. I can have him run out of the service as unfit." He spoke softly.

The night seemed to wait around them. The grass was fuzzy in its wetness.

"Let it go," pleaded the boy. "He's got just a few months left before he retires."

There was a little smirk from Callan and he did not take his eyes from Henneken, and Swanson stared at the sleeping man in the sordid wetness of the grass and the night with its rain was suddenly as still as the waiting of a heartbeat, as still as the moment before the falling of fruit, and as he spoke he felt a great rushing collapse. "Would you do it for me?"

"For you?" He turned as if amazed, incredulous. For a moment he stared at the boy and then slowly he began to smile. "For you," he repeated. He looked back at Henneken, as one might look at a prize, and from his throat came a little humming sound. His boot inched toward the partially exposed stomach and Swanson, in beginning terror, had a sudden image of a cat lying dead on the road.

And the sergeant's foot lifted and kneaded the belly, ever so gently. "Maybe," he said. "Maybe this time I'll let it go."

Chapter Eleven

Aldous Brown had a way about him when he talked, a way of groping and stumbling for words, as if some natural honesty prevented an easier glibness. One night he came and sat at the edge of Swanson's bunk. "I been thinkin," he said, and he looked down at his boots. "You ain't been goin to town so much any more."

"It's been raining."

"Yeah. Even 'fore the rain though, you was kinda slowin down."

"It's pretty busy around here now."

"You don't have no trouble with you girl?"

"How'd you know I had a girl?"

The Negro chuckled, as if he were already happy to be beginning a conversation. "Well, now, that's something you can just smell."

"You're all right, Aldous." He hesitated. "I've been going into town a long time, long before I had a girl. I don't think it's that," he said vaguely.

Aldous's manner became serious again, tentative. "Ain't nobody likes this place. But they gets

used to it bein bad and it gets comfortable as a pig
pen an they afraid to go away."

Swanson liked the Negro's slow kind of insight.
He raised himself slightly from the bunk and
looked at the others around the room. Pop Henneken was sitting in his usual spot near the stove
and he watched the old man as he spoke. "It
doesn't seem to get you down, Aldous. You seem
pretty square with things."

"It get me down plenty. I'm thinkin all the time
what to do 'bout it. I tell you somethin," and he
spoke with a peculiar reserve. "You know what I
do? I ride a bike. Thas all. I rent myself a bike in
the village an go for a ride . . . sometimes all
week end, just peddlin away an on Saturday night
I stop in some village where there ain't no soldiers
and I drink a little vin blanc . . . but the peddlin
is the thing." He paused, rather shy with his ad-
mission. "But you, you is the one, you is the real
killer. Goin all the time to town. I never seen
many what did that," he said admiringly. "You
was about the only one," he added, and there was
no taint in his using of the past tense. "I used to
shake my head every time I see you leavin. All
dressed up in them French clothes! Jus a young
stud on his way to a ball. Yeah. You don't know
what made you stop goin?"

"I don't know." He put his hands behind his
head and already his first desire to talk was fad-
ing.

"Maybe it's workin for that man."

Swanson took a cigarette from the pocket of his

fatigue jacket. He lighted it without changing his position on the bunk.

"I been wantin to ask you how it is in that office. You's kind of touchy 'bout it, ain't you? I figured maybe you thought there was some of us sore with you for takin the job but there ain't, not that I know. It's the best job in the company, I'd say, you gotta be jealous not to say it. An hell, it ain't the free world, a man's got to take a job when the top sergeant makes the order."

"He didn't order me to take the job."

"Yeah? You figure it was a better deal?"

"No." He smoked his cigarette nervously. He didn't see any way to explain it. He couldn't explain it to himself.

"Well," the Negro said more slowly, "it don't make no difference."

"Yes it does."

Aldous Brown reached down and scratched his leg. He seemed to be considering. He seemed careful with the moment. Swanson sat up suddenly. "Listen, what do you think of that man? Tell me as best you can say."

"Well, like I said, when he first come I knows there was bad in him. He's a good soldier, I says, but he's bad mean. It don't always show up. You got to look for it. An sometime you try and lean his way an you tell yourself he's not doin nothin but his duty. But then you see things."

"What things?" said Swanson.

"Well, jus' the way he is mean with the men."

Swanson nodded. For a time he didn't speak

and he smoked his cigarette and stared at the blanket covering his bunk. He dropped the cigarette into a butt can and looked up at the Negro. "Anything else?"

"What about? Him?"

"No. No, nothing."

After a while Aldous Brown got up from the bunk to warm his hands by the stove. Swanson turned on his side so that he faced the wall. Talk was no good anyhow, he thought. It couldn't dissolve the weight inside him. Maybe it made it worse, all the words lingering and nervous on the outside with never enough weight to touch in.

He lay on his bunk facing the wall until he heard Pop Henneken get up and shuffle through the door. The thought of the old man caused another quick tightening in his chest. Why was it he had stood up for him like that? It wasn't his business what Callan did or what happened to Pop. But when he'd seen him curled in the weeds . . . it had been frightening. It was still frightening. The wet night, the look on Callan's face. . . . It had been almost like seeing himself lying there helpless.

I don't want to get like this, he kept thinking. . . . I don't want to get like this. Presently, when Aldous or Sam had switched out the light he got up from the bunk and went out into the wet night. Only a few of the huts were dark. Callan's hut was one of them and when he walked up and glanced into the window of the Orderly room he could see he wasn't there. It was empty save for the CQ, a soldier from the depot who sat at one of the desks reading a comic book.

He went back down the company street until he was at the edge of the meadow. I'm going to see Solange, he thought. When the weather dries up I'm going to see her no matter how I feel.

As he wandered toward the noise of the enlisted men's club he tried to absorb himself in the thought of the girl. I know how she is, he mused. She'd rather have me feeling lousy in front of her than going off to hide it. Hiding it doesn't make me any better. It doesn't mean I'm any stronger.

The outside of the club was deserted, the window counter closed. A light drizzle gave the patio a dark shine and he stood dry against the wall and felt the current of talk from within. He listened but the voices were too blurred to be recognized.

He moved around to the entrance and stood for a moment before entering. When he pushed through the door he went across the crowded room with his eyes lowered and waited his turn at the plank bar.

He ordered his beer and sat at a corner table with the can cupped in front of him. The talk was a hum, a cushion. He sat as quiet as he could and then he knew he had been listening and that he'd heard what he had listened for. The voice was distinct, unmistakable above the others, and it shamed him to realize he had waited for it. He had wanted to know where Callan was and it shamed him.

He looked up slowly. Callan was seated at a full

table across the room, hunched forward, talking loudly with several men from another company and he watched as from a dark audience, as if the man were terribly in the distance. He seemed naked as a red-faced doll, his actions as he talked seeming unreal away from the closeness of the Orderly room.

"Ain't it the truth," he heard him say, and when the voice drowned beneath someone's burst of laughter he could see it only like a pantomime, the face twisted in red expression, the tough hands strangely graceful as they caressed the muted words. He had never heard him use "ain't" before, nor seen such fullness in his gestures. Callan's drunk, he thought, and he was frightened with his own fascination.

He made himself sip from the can to break from the watching.

When he raised his eyes the sergeant was looking at him.

There was a slow delight in the sergeant's expression, delight with himself, as if an instinct had been confirmed. He smiled and then his shout burst through the din of the club. "C'mere, Swanson!"

He imagined the whole room turning toward him, a great hush in the echo of the sergeant's voice.

"Swanson, by God, c'mere." With a stiff wave Callan was demanding him to the table.

As if propelled, he stood up and walked across the room, his temples pulsing with each step.

He was not fully aware of the sergeant's greeting him, pulling him down like an old friend into an open seat beside him. And then he realized that the men around the table were nodding and that the sergeant was making some kind of elaborate introduction. "It's Private First Class Swanson, gentlemen, a young man with great sensitivities. Look at him, gentlemen. He's usually in town by this time but tonight he's staying in. I should say!" He laughed, and as he spoke he fawned over the boy, red-faced, exuding a kind of weaving force.

Dimly he heard the sergeant launch again into conversation, something about the horses of the old Cavalry, and the men at the table were laughing often, and Callan turned toward him with each flare of laughter, as if to point out his ability to be appreciated. The talk went on in the distance and more often the sergeant turned toward him, until finally the conversation washed by and he was being spoken to quietly, confidential, the drunk eyes focused intentfully.

"How are yuh, boy? You never talk to me, what's wrong, don't you like the old sarge? Sure, no reason to stand off like that. Listen, how'd you like some good scotch? I'd say you'd like that, huh? Listen now, I got some in my hut and I'm going to run get it and you and me can sneak out for a little drink. No use being sore at each other alla time. Just wait here, don't move, and I'm going to run get it."

He heard the sergeant's voice as out of a bad dream and he was still fuzzy with a black embarrassment, unable to bring together his thoughts. He stared dumbly at the man's perspiring face. "I was leaving," he managed.

"Leaving? What'd you come in for if it wasn't for a drink? Tell me that, huh?"

He shook his head, conscious of the sudden quiet at the table.

"What's wrong, Swanson?" said the sergeant, and his mood became happy and childish in the new quiet. "You don't want to treat the old sarge like a bum. We oughta be friends, my God! Work together all day, don't we? Oughta relax a little, have some fun. I'm not such a bad guy, not like you think."

Smiling, he straightened in his chair and waited until the table talk sprang up again, joining in with a grunt, a laugh. Then he leaned back, his tone for just the two of them. "If I was such a bad guy wouldn't I of had old Henneken court-martialed? I didn't, did I? How is he? How is old Pop?"

There was no change from the innocence of his expression. "Some of 'em go bad like that at his age. But I figured, you know that time, well I figured, what the hell, he's only got a few months to go, I'll give him a break, see if I can get him by so's he'll get his retirement."

Swanson couldn't answer. If he could tear loose from the hollow pull of the chair, rip loose and be away, outside, away, anywhere in the coldness of the night. The man's closeness held him. And through it all ran a fear, not for Henneken or anyone else, but a fear like electricity, personal, rol-

ing inside him like an echo to the sergeant's innocence.

"Now you listen," broke in the voice, hushed,
pleased, "you know where I got that scotch? Right
out of the captain's car, that's where. And what's
he going to say, what's he going to do? Nothing.
It's illegal to have hard liquor in his car, so's he
going to report it missing?" He tapped Swanson's
knee. "I'll bet he knows I got it. So what?" He
smiled. "He's scared of me."

He spoke in a half-whisper, hunched forward,
his eyes gleaming as to an accomplice. And as
quickly he cooled, sharpened. "I'm going to get
that scotch now so you wait here." He turned back
to the men around the table. "You watch this
boy," he said boisterously. He seemed happily
drunk. "Don't let him get away." He stood up and
put a hand on Swanson's shoulder, as if to keep
him in the chair. "Watch him," he repeated, and
he lurched off across the crowded room.

Out of the heat came the thought that he must
get up and go. No, that was wrong, it would make
it worse. Not now, he told himself, not like an es-
cape. His body ached with wanting to leave. But
he kept himself in the chair.

In a matter of minutes Callan reappeared, the
bottle bulging beneath his khaki shirt. He pointed
toward Swanson as he sat down. "It's my company
clerk and him and me is gonna have a business
talk. Best time in the world to talk business—over
a drink. Yes sir! C'mon Swans, we're gonna leave
these here lechers, all they want is the old sarge's

whisky." He stood again, weaving slightly, more as from excitement than from drunkenness. "C'mon," he repeated, searching over the room as if to determine an exit. His hand was on the boy's arm, pulling him up, and then Swanson was walking ahead quickly, the feel of the sergeant's hand on his back.

When they were outside, Swanson continued across the patio, quickening his step until he felt the hand drop and heard the man's pace recede behind his own. "This is good right here," came the voice over his shoulder. But he kept walking, rapidly. "Swanson!" came the shout. He moved farther into the night and the voice in its growing distance was even louder. "I mean it!"

And suddenly, almost running, he felt ridiculous. He stopped and listened to the beat of his own heart. Why am I doing this? he thought. He waited for his breathing to slow. What was happening to him? A grown man! And how often lately had he called himself that, sarcastically. Why was he here, half on the run? What was he thinking of?

He made himself turn around. There was the sergeant's figure, forlorn at the edge of the patio, the bulge still discernible beneath his shirt.

"I mean it," came the call again, softer, and there was something pathetic to the voice.

He walked back to where the man was standing alone. Callan bent his head and motioned toward the patio chairs. "This is good enough," he muttered. "We can sit here."

"All right, Sergeant."

They sat down and Callan took the bottle out of his shirt. "You think I don't like you. Huh?"

He shrugged his shoulders. His running off would not be mentioned, he knew it curiously, and it made him feel a bit of sorrow for the man.

"I guess maybe it's because it's hard to know me," said Callan. He seemed suddenly quiet and humble. He opened the scotch and offered it and after a pause Swanson tilted the bottle and felt the first whisky going warm down his throat. When he handed it back Callan held it for a moment on his lap. He seemed to be thinking. Then he took a long swallow.

"I been twenty-six years in the service," he said quietly. He looked down at the cement of the patio. "I only weighed a hundred and two pounds when I came in, sixteen years old and a hundred and two pounds. I wasn't like you. Maybe you think you got the world by the ass because you're a tall kid, pretty good-looking and all that. I don't know if you think that or not, maybe not. No, I guess you don't," he said without looking up. "I wouldn't like you if you did.

"I only weighed a hundred and two but that don't mean that anyone gave me any shit. I hope to tell yuh, nobody fooled with me, not even then. I did my work and they did theirs and I got somewhere. The youngest sergeant in the regiment, that's what I was. The old Forty-first, it was the Cavalry in those days. I coulda been an officer, I coulda had a commission during the war. I ain't

a dummy, Swanson, maybe you think I am. You
look at the records. I know all about IQs and the
stuff the punks are always talkin about. You look
at mine sometime, it's right there on the records,
as high as anybody's. Maybe my speech ain't as
good as yours but it could be if I wanted it to."

He gulped another drink from the bottle. He
looked away into the night, his eyes dull in heavy
reflection. "In the war I was a hero," he said. "I
got the DSC. Right here in France. Near Tours."

There was a pause between each sentence, almost poetic, and he lifted his head slightly, his
chin tilted up and profiled to the night. The bottle
hung loosely from his hand. His cheeks had a spe-
cial red to them, beyond the drinking. The dullness left his eyes and they glistened as to music, as
in a reverie. And then he spoke quietly, proudly.
"When I was young the officers used to want me
near them. I could be walking by myself, only
seventeen or eighteen I was, and I could walk by
battalion headquarters and they'd call out to me.
They were just standing there in the evening, a
bunch of officers outside of headquarters. They'd
call out to me and I'd go over and stand around
with them and they might introduce me, 'You
know Private Callan, don't you, a good soldier, a
good little soldier.' Maybe one of them would put
a hand on my shoulder and they'd go right on talking, just having me there."

He turned, his face glowing from the remem-
brance, his breathing very deep and slow and regu-

lar. "And I like you, Swanson, so help me God."

Swanson sank into his chair and turned so that he faced away. "How about another drink?"

The bottle was handed slowly, resentful. "What's wrong, ain't my talk good enough for you?"

"Sure. Of course," he said quickly. "Look, you're a funny guy." It was too quick, he knew, the wrong thing. He tried to cover it. "Do you mind being in a Quartermaster unit?"

"What do you mean, funny guy?"

"Hell, nothing. I was thinking about how it would be for you, the change to the Quartermaster."

"So I'm a funny guy, huh? You mean a man can't get drunk and talk a little without somebody watching him or calling him nuts." And suddenly he was hard, knowing. "You don't like me saying I like you, that's it, ain't it? All right, I don't like yuh, how's that? I think you're a snot-nosed kid, how's that?"

His face was changing over into rage and with a desperate casualness the boy leaned forward and slapped his shoulder. "Hell, you must be drunk all right." He laughed as he looked into the red face. "Hell, I was just trying to talk to you."

The sergeant hesitated, peering at him intently.

"Sure I'm glad you like me," said the boy. "I thought you had it in for me."

Callan sat back in his chair and after a moment he took another drink from the bottle. "Nah," he said. He sat thinking. "No, uh-uh," he mumbled.

"And I didn't mean what I just said. I just get sore like that."

"Sure, I know."

"I didn't mean it at all. No sir." He wagged his head in drunken, serious denial and Swanson knew, as he watched him, what was coming next. He knew it with a warm shame.

"I meant the first thing I said, because I do like yuh. It's hard for me to like a person but when I like 'em I like 'em and that's it. Those guys in there"—he gestured toward the noise of the club—"I don't give a shit for the run-of-the-mill guy. But you're different. You've got good stuff in you, boy."

"That's nice of you to say." Slowly, he stood up.

The sergeant reached out and placed a hand on the boy's foot. "Let me tell you something. We're gonna be partners, buddies. I told you I liked you and I mean it. That's all there is to it. We're gonna be together just like a team."

Swanson felt his spine long and clamped. He did not answer.

"You're not leavin, are yuh, with all this liquor left?" He swallowed once more from the bottle and he stood up beside the boy. "At least you can walk the old sarge home." His mouth was hanging in a grin. "Good strong arm, that's what I need." He lurched against the boy, almost sliding to the ground. "C'mon. That's it. Let the old sarge get an arm around yuh."

With the sergeant against him Swanson started

for the company area. He walked with the man lurching beside him and sometimes the head dropped heavily onto his shoulder. He tried not to think of him. He suspected he was not as drunk as he walked. A tinge, a quick wave of nausea passed over him. He knew the man was not that drunk.

When they reached the sergeant's hut he undid himself and Callan leaned up against the wall as if he were helpless. "We made it," he mumbled, eyes half-closed. "Ol' Swans. I knew he'd bring us through."

"I'm going now, Sergeant. I'll see you tomorrow."

Callan straightened himself against the wall, coming to life. He seemed about to protest. Instead, as though chilled by some thought, he offered his hand and spoke quietly, almost sober. "Goodnight, pal." He held the grip, and his eyes brightened again until they were nearly moist. "Buddy," he said, urging it. "Old buddy."

Swanson turned and walked back across the gravel street. It was not until he had reached his own hut that he heard Callan's door closing. He lay on his bunk without undressing, his head pushed into the gray hollow of the pillow. He thought about going into town, about the rain ending and how he must get out of the camp and go into town. It was a thought that repeated like a fever. He lay fully clothed on his bunk and as he strained to sleep he felt he was rocking with the stove and its nervous, moving heat.

Chapter Twelve

For a day and a night it did not rain and on the second day the sky eased into a splotched, precarious blue. The wooden sidewalks stretched back into a splintered dryness and the humped gravel of the streets took on a new and warmer shine.

At the camp football field Swanson threw warm-up passes to three men from his company. The field was no more than a cleared lot, soggy still with a rich mud, and before each pass he wiped his hands down across his fatigue pants. Aldous Brown trotted in from downfield, pointing to the crowd that milled along the sidelines.

"Thas a real audience this time."

Swanson nodded.

"We can take these here engineers."

"Sure," he said flatly.

"C'mon man. You got to get excited 'bout these thing. Thas what make it good."

Swanson nodded and tossed a short pass to Ivy, the stove-keeper.

"I bet all you thinkin 'bout is gettin this game ova and takin that pass."

"Damn rights that's all I'm thinking about." He tried to make a joke of it by smiling but the first vehement truth of it had already escaped.

And it was the truth, a day and night truth, his only thought or hope in the past week. In the afternoon Callan had handed him the memo that lifted the restriction on passes. As he had tacked it to the bulletin board he had had to tighten his body, tighten it physically to hold down the dark burst of relief. And even now, with one pass after another, even now he could feel the tightness. He could think of Callan and how it had been worse since that night on the patio. The way he had come into the office on the following morning . . . the footsteps coming down the wooden walk, the banging of the door, then the wordless walk to his desk. And the morning had gone like that, without a word or a glance. He had known it was going to be like that. He had known it before he heard the footsteps on the wooden walk. He suffered through the morning silence and he knew that Callan's only thought was of the evening before. He could glimpse the man's head bent rigid over his work, coiled, as if he could draw back the night into the curl of his body.

And he had sat there opposite the man and he could picture those eyes of the evening before, their bright urgency. And Callan could know that the picture was there.

He had spoken to the man, spoken to burst the

building air. A favor he had asked, if he could
leave for several minutes to pick up shirts from the
laundry. He could hear himself as he spoke and the
beat of his own heart. Callan started, recoiled at
the sound of his voice and then he understood the
meaning of the words, that he was being asked a
favor, and he stared across, repeating the question
as if to give his own reactions time. "The laundry?
You want to go to the laundry?" He paused and
his hands came around into square fists and he
leaned forward with cheeks that squinted with a
relieved and ready hate. "Don't you ask me any
favors!" It was a hiss, paced, clipped. "You don't
move!"

And he had known it would be like that, and yet
the knowing did not ease the strain. He had to get
away. He kept throwing passes, throwing as quickly
as the ball was returned to him.

A referee in a white sweatshirt came out from
the sidelines and blew his whistle and they lined
up for the kickoff. As he stood waiting he looked
over the hundred or so men on the sidelines. Callan was there, standing off at the far end of the
field. He was in his slicker after two days without
rain.

He played badly for the first half hour. There
was no scoring in the heavy mud, and it was not
until the second half that he tried a pass. He could
hear the warming shouts as they spread back to
cover his receivers and he spotted Aldous Brown
cutting into the clear and he tossed it soft and
arching and the Negro dived forward, slapping the

ball upward, then gathering it in frantically as he slipped down into the mud. On the sidelines a roar of appreciation rose from the partisan rooters. The Negro got up and trotted back with a stony expression, breaking into an embarrassed grin as he drew up to them. "Great catch!" said Tom.

"Naw, it was the pass. You gotta have it to throw one with that slippery ball."

"Pass hell, it was a great catch."

They went back into a huddle and he knelt down inside the globe they made, his fingers tracing a plan in the mud. The mud was all right, he thought. He felt like sloshing in it, getting good and dirty, good and worked out and afterward there would be plenty of hot water and then into Bordeaux to see Solange. He was feeling better. "Let's try it again," he said. "Go out to the right, Aldous, then cut clear across." He motioned toward Ivy. "You take off on the left and go straight out."

They broke the huddle and the others moved ahead to form the line and he waited for the snap from center. In the second before it came he knew that he felt better than he had in days, elated even, alone, tipping on the verge of the motion of the play. He wanted the feel of the ball in his palms. There was a tingling in his thighs and a good anticipation across the flatness of his stomach. This was his business, all him. And he took the snap from center and he was conscious of himself drifting back from the grunting line play. Downfield,

Aldous Brown was cutting diagonally, and from part of his eye he saw two men charging him but he took his time and threw flat and rapid into the Negro's jumping chest. The linemen hit and he was down into the mud and as he rolled over and stood again he could see Aldous free and crossing the goal. Suddenly the play seemed without parts, all one fine motion filled with a clean and easy excitement.

The game ended six to nothing and they filed off the field with a loose tiredness. They passed by where Callan was standing and Callan singled him out with an expressionless stare. "Hello athalete," he said quietly.

It affected his good feeling as he went toward the showers. He couldn't tell if it was a compliment or some kind of insult.

After a shower and clean clothes he went to the Orderly room for his pass. The sergeant was at his desk, working over his fingernails with a toothpick. "Where you going?" he said.

"Into town." He began to write his name in the pass book.

"No more passes for you."

"What?" He looked up from the pass book and his hand was hollow and rubbery. The sergeant continued to work the toothpick beneath his nails, glancing up into Swanson's startled face, his own face blank as if nothing further need be said.

"What do you mean?"

Callan shrugged his shoulders. "That's right, it's

an order. No more passes for you." He got up casually and walked past Swanson out of the Orderly
room.

The pencil was still suspended in his hand and
he set it down like a hot thing. He stood partly
stunned over the pass book. Then he turned and
ran out of the office. The sergeant was walking
short-legged and slow toward his hut. He caught
up and side-stepped clumsily beside him. "I can't
understand this. What is it with you that you've got
to do this?"

The sergeant stopped abruptly. "Don't talk to
me, boy." The "boy" had a thick personal sound.

Callan walked on, and shamefully he dragged
beside him. "But what's the object in it? Why are
you cutting off my passes?" He hated the tone of
his own voice; he could feel himself as a pleading
child.

The sergeant turned into his hut and Swanson
followed and watched tightly as the man sat on his
bunk and began to remove his boots. His body was
swaying in its tightness. Presently Callan looked
up, mild, unconcerned. At the corners of his
mouth there were small relaxed creases. "Don't
come around me. I gave you an order."

Swanson clenched his fists to the silence and the
sergeant went back to removing his boots. The boy
hovered there, sick with his own desperateness.
And then he lost all care and he wanted only to go
on, plunge into it. "The policy is to allow overnight
passes to anyone who wants one."

For a moment Callan continued to unlace his
boots. Then he looked up slowly. "I make the pol-
icies," he said softly. His face took on a queer patience. "You've been taking too many passes,
Swanson. Some silly-ass French girl is running you
ragged in Bordeaux. You're coming in late and it
interferes with your work."

"You said my work was good."

"I've changed my mind."

"What . . . How long before I can have a pass?"

"When I think you're ready for one." He smiled.
He set his boots neatly beneath his bunk and lay
down, looking up at the boy. "Now why are you
getting all upset? It doesn't look well, a big solid
athalete like you."

Swanson stood with his finger tips touching
lightly against his pants, but his fingers were rigid
and the muscles in his arms were shaking. It was a
physical struggle to turn and leave the hut. He
went back to the Orderly room and sat alone at
his desk. Outside, it was beginning to be evening.
He rapped his palm against the desk. He sat back
and tried to think of nothing. His mind worked
more painfully and rapidly than ever. He saw the
picture of himself pleading with Callan, and thinking of it stirred a heat that ran up his legs and
filled his chest. There was the man's coarse face, its
awful composure. He shook himself as though to cast
off the scene. He put his head into his hands, staring
into the darkness of his palms. Then he could feel
his eyelids wet and his palms wet and he knew he

was going to lay his face into the cool wood of the desk.

The door slammed and he heard the CQ saying "Hiya, Swanson," and he kept his palms to his face as if he were tired or in thought. He turned his back and dropped his hands and the moisture was naked all over his eyes and cheeks. "Hiya," he returned, his back to the newcomer, and then he couldn't keep it up and he stumbled out of the office with the tears streaming down his face.

Chapter Thirteen

He couldn't talk with the men in the hut. He couldn't bring himself to tell of the restriction. About it all there was something so personal and close that in thinking of it he would turn away from the others, he would lie fully clothed on the top of his bunk, his face toward the bumpy, splintered, whitewashed wall, and the world would become as small as the hunch of his body into the fuzz of the blanket.

Each night he tried to write a letter to Solange. He sat with pencil and paper on his foot locker and the words wouldn't come. He wanted to tell her why he couldn't see her; he wanted to explain what he had felt the day he had left her on the street. He couldn't do it. It hurt him, a tight hurting darkness, and as he sat with pencil and paper it would get worse and then he would throw aside the pencil and slip onto the bunk.

One night he forced himself to finish and send a letter, and it was bad, no more than a spurting apology.

The men in the hut, mostly they left him alone. They were sharp to any change and they could feel his difference. They were reluctant to address him. They found themselves forming sentences in their minds before speaking to him and when they spoke it would be flat and precarious. "What is it with you?" Sam ventured once.

The boy looked at him, blankly, and turned away.

A few days after he sent the letter he went to the mail room and there was a little blue envelope with her name in the corner. He took it back to the hut and waited until the others were occupied.

Dear Tom,
I was relieved to get your note and it was silly of you to think that I was angry, although I admit I was very worried. I thought perhaps you were ill. I know being restricted is very difficult for you but I'm sure that it will work itself out. Of course I will be happy to see you any time when you are free.
                              Yours,
                                  Solange

When he was finished reading he folded the letter and put it into his shirt pocket. It did not make him feel any better. It's short, he thought, just a note. Yet it was not much shorter than what he had written to her. What had he expected? Sympathy? Did he want her to come falling all over him with sugary phrases of comfort? He took the letter from his pocket and reread it. She's good, he told himself. She's good and fair and understanding.

He went over each word of the note but more and more it seemed cold and like a rejection. She doesn't care, he thought. He held the letter helplessly between his legs and then he had to stop himself from crumbling it in his fist. He went over to his wall locker and placed it inside on the top shelf and then he stared aimlessly at his uniforms and personal effects.

Aldous Brown came over by the locker and stood next to him, peering in. "I got some soap like that." He reached in after a bar of green-wrapped Palmolive soap, examining it as if it were a miraculous thing. "Yes sir, I got a bar just like that!" Clownlike, he gaped at Swanson.

For a moment Swanson stared blankly and then he blinked the dumbness out of his eyes and made an effort to smile.

"Well now," said Aldous. He tossed the soap back and began to snap his fingers to an imaginary tune. "Nothin's bad. Nothin's really bad, no sir!"

"I guess not," said Swanson. He tried to direct a smile around the room, but he felt the thinness of it and he turned away from Aldous and picked his cap from the foot of his bunk and left the hut.

He thought of the girl as he walked out of the company area into the larger darkness of the camp. Since that moment after the football field he had not been able to see her clearly. It was muddled, meshed, twisted so that none of it seemed real. She's through with me, he thought, and he knew he was being unreasonable but he went ahead with it anyway. She's through with me and

I don't blame her and I couldn't even look at her
if we came face to face. And why not? Why not?
he persisted, and when he sat down at the edge of
the meadow the flesh of his cheeks was like an
animal's, twitching to the touch of hovering insects, and he tried to quiet himself by placing his
hands gently over his face, but there was nothing
but the redness of not being able to follow along
with his thoughts.

Solange. She was only one girl. There were a lot
of girls. In the woods across the meadow there
were a dozen whores. They were girls, weren't
they? Already he'd seen the shadows of men moving toward them through the night, and he
watched and thought of himself.

The only time he had been with a whore was
when he had first gotten overseas, when the transport train had stopped for a three-hour layover
in Paris. And it had been a bad experience. But
I've done all right with girls, he thought quickly,
and he eased somewhat as he went back over the
times. What was the first girl's name? He couldn't
remember. But she was the only one besides the
whore that he had felt badly about. He couldn't
remember her name but he could see, again, her
face, her features. She was sixteen, his age. In the
beginning she wanted to, she kept telling him she
loved him and would do anything for him, but
then she had begun to cry and she cried afterward,
too, and he remembered her crying face and the
way she said she never wanted to go home again,
she could never face her parents. He sat with her

in the car trying to tell her it was all right and that it wasn't bad, and the more he had tried to convince her the worse he felt himself.

But with Gelda it had been different. How old was he then? Seventeen? And she was two years older, nineteen. She was a big girl and she laughed a lot and he would never forget her looks, the look of her summer-tanned body and the look of her large even teeth that showed so white and healthy when she laughed. She was sitting next to him in a movie; it was dark, but he could tell she was pretty by the way she was laughing, so easy but not silly, and they started to comment on the movie together and afterward he took her out for a hamburger. Then the next night he borrowed his father's car and they drove out and parked somewhere in the country, turning to each other when he first shut off the ignition, just letting it go natural and without stopping. She didn't cry before or after or any time, but kept kissing him and laughing a little, telling him that he was one of the sweetest boys she'd ever known but that she was kind of bad herself because she was engaged to be married in a month and if it weren't for that she would rather be with him every night than anyone in the world.

As he thought of her, sitting there on the damp earth of the meadow, he had to smile. Even now she made him feel better. Comfortable. And there was something he had learned from her—not to push too hard, not to strain in having a girl, because then it wasn't real any more, it turned into

something else. It had to be right for both of them,
ready . . . then his heart would go with it and
then it was good. It was something he believed.
For him he knew it was right, because after Gelda
there had been some others and with each of them
there was a better feeling afterward than before.

But it hadn't been any good with the whore.
Everybody had been drunk and crazy during those
three hours in Paris. They'd all left the train and
spread out looking for women. He had taken his
to a hotel room that was bare except for a bed and
sink, and she was undressed first and she went and
lay on the bed and motioned to him. And suddenly
his excitement had collapsed into the emptiness of
the room. He had gone ahead, but it was like doing
something he had to do. When he dressed and left
the room he couldn't get back to that first zest of
stepping off the train. He felt heavy. He kept
thinking of the whore. The only picture in his
mind was of her waiting on the bed, smiling that
startling fixed smile. And as he walked heavily
through the Paris streets he knew what it was that
hurt him most: the indifference. The indifference
of it and the change that made, that other quality
it inspired, so that he seemed to be watching himself. He didn't want anything unless it was part
of a good flow, the next real step after the last.

But why did he have to think of all that now?
Again and again in the past week he had gone over
these same things. He put his face back into his
hands, as though to close off the redness.

From a few yards off came the sound of a man

coughing. He looked ahead and saw a figure sitting, darker than the night. "Who is it?" he called.
There was no answer. "Who's there?" He got up
and moved closer. He didn't mind if he had to
rouse the man up, he wanted to plunge himself
into something, anything. "Who is it?" he challenged. He walked directly to where the figure was
humped in the grass and Pop Henneken, the old
man, looked up to him with a smile that was silly
and innocent. He was holding a wine bottle across
his lap and another one lay empty by his side.

"You gonna have a drink with Pop?" said the old
man.

The aggressiveness slipped from him and in a
strange way, almost sorrowful, he was glad to see
Pop Henneken. In all the months they had lived
together they had hardly spoken, but now he
looked down at the old man and he was sorry.

"Sure I'll have a drink." He sat down in the
grass and accepted the bottle that weaved toward
him. "I'd like to have a drink!"

The old man watched him drink, his purple lips
in a soft smile, the old brown eyes like wet glass.
Then he sighed. "It's a shitty life. It's a shitty life,
Tom." He was addressing the boy and even in his
drunkenness, even through the profanity, his tone
was oddly respectful. "You think badly of old Pop,
don't you?" he said, then slowly he nodded his
head, affirming his own words. "You think he's a
drunk old bastard. And you're right."

"Nah," mumbled Swanson.

"Yes you do. I don't blame you."

The boy swallowed another drink and the old man took the bottle and set it upright on the ground between them. His wizened mouth was tilted philosophically and he seemed content, having the boy with him. "I can't help it though, I swear I can't. I been so long in this life. Ah, this shitty life." As he swore again his head stopped its weaving, as if the profanity gave him strength. "Nineteen years I been in this Army, nineteen long long years. I figured always I'd do twenty and retire, just have a hundred, hundred-twenty-five a month an do somethin nice and quiet, just do what I want. Always thought I'd do twenty and now it's all over. It's all finished now." He shook his head.

"Sure you'll do twenty. What do you mean?"

"Never, not now, no no. He's gonna get me. He'll get me for sure."

Swanson looked away into the night. "Who?" he said.

"The sergeant." The old man took another drink, putting his hand on the ground behind for support. The night was cold and dark, a shiver night. The old man paused and seemed to suck in with sorrow. "He'll get me, I know it. Maybe he don't have to but he will. I'm just an old drunk is all, but it's funny how you get to know things when you're drunk. You feel things for sure."

Swanson reached out for the wine bottle and took a long drink. He was conscious of his eyes' being open as he swallowed.

"You been feeling bad lately," said Pop. "We

can tell how you're feeling bad, and it makes a
man sorry. But for you I ain't scared. It don't matter what you're feeling bad about cause it's gonna
pass. I always knew about you. You're fresh and
young and strong an there ain't a better man in
the company."

"No. Don't say that."

"Ain't nothin wrong in it, it's the truth.
Nothin's gonna bother you, not for long. Always
fulla life, that's what, ain't complainin alla time.
You got the stuff to be a leader, an officer if you
wanted."

Swanson shook his head and continued to drink
from the bottle.

"Guys got respect for you. That's somethin you
can tell."

"I'm no better off than anybody else."

"Yes you are. Yes sir." The old man's mouth
dropped, but his head was rigid as if he were fixed
with the idea. "You're one fellah who's gonna
make it."

Swanson's head throbbed slightly. He lifted the
remainder of the wine to his lips, not thinking to
share it, then he set down the bottle and stared
out at the distant flicker of campfires in the wood.
Even with the alcohol his body was heavy, dead-
ened.

After a while Pop said, "But it ain't no use for
me. I ain't cryin. I just know it, that's all."

Swanson stared down at the wet grass between
his legs. "You can get by, Pop," he muttered.
"Just try, that's the thing. He doesn't have to get

you." And as he spoke he could feel his thoughts begin to center and suddenly he was clear and excited. He jerked toward the older man with words tumbling one after the other. "Just try, Pop, you've got to! You can get by that man, I know you can. Listen to me!" he cried. "You've got to fight!"

The old man looked startled. He made an elaborate shrug with his thin shoulders and peered curiously at the empty bottle on the ground. Tensely, Swanson watched him. The old eyes wandered in drunkenness, dull, forgetful.

"Pop!" He tried to hold him with the intensity of his own feeling.

"Huh," replied the drooping head. The thin frame leaned to one side, hanging there, and a fuzzy, cord-veined hand reached out to touch the ground, lightly, testing its moisture in an unconscious way. Swanson leaned toward him and whispered hoarsely, "You're listening, aren't you, you've got to fight!"

But the old man didn't answer. His head inched downward. Almost like a child he let himself to the ground, tenderly, his legs neatly together, the knees pushed up near his stomach.

Swanson hovered over him, shocked. He reached out and grasped a bony shoulder, shaking it, but there was only a soft grunt of protest. Desperately he sat on beside him. "Dammit! Dammit to hell!" He put his hands to his cheeks, wiping them hard. "Get up, Pop," he pleaded, speaking out to the whole darkness of the night. "C'mon Pop, get up for me." The old man wheezed steadily where he lay.

Now Swanson could feel his own drunkenness. He picked up one of the bottles and hurled it out into the meadow. With clumsy purpose he got to his feet, standing above the sleeping figure, then turning away from it as from a discarded thing. He moved a few steps, stumbling in the soft, false-bottomed grass. "I'll get me a whore." The quick thought formed itself in the soldier's vernacular. "That's it, by God, I'll get me a whore."

Drunkenly, he plodded out through the meadow toward the depth of the wood. "Make her right there under the trees, by God. Won't let her take me anywhere, just right there in the goddamn bushes. Christ yes. Ream her out. Give it to her good!" He pushed out through the wet meadow, his arms churning stiffly at his sides, and when his foot plunged through the earth into a cushion of slime he yanked it out with a squishing sound. Frantically he moved through the dark. "Goddamn right," he breathed like a tempo, like a beat to his stumbling motion.

Then he fell and picked himself up and fell again. He lay face down in the sucking moisture. It was soft and warm-wet against his thighs and chest and face. He lay there as in a coma, a terrible pause. "Good Christ," he whispered. "I don't have to do this. I don't have to get like this."

He struggled to pull himself up. He had to get his chest free of the ground so he wouldn't feel the beat of his heart. Even then he could hear it, a great hollow thumping high in his chest. He stared about and there was nothing anywhere. The floor of the meadow was black. The straight-ahead sky was black. He sank into the mud with a low, pleading moan, and he sank deep and wretched into its holding comfort.

He knew after some moments that he was out past the boundary that marked the limits of the camp. If an MP came through the meadow he would be found and he'd have to show a pass. "And so I don't have a pass. I don't have a pass and I've broken his restriction." A wave of amazement made it easier for him to think. He'd like it, me getting like this. He'd like it if I was caught, he thought, amazed, awed.

In a frenzy he forced himself to his feet and began to stumble toward the camp, pushing on blindly until the ground became harder and sandy and then he knew that he was back across the line. Again, he slipped back onto the earth. He didn't have to go any farther. He could stay there all night if he wanted. He lay down on the ground. He wanted to stay there all night. He wanted to tuck his hand between the tightness of his thighs with his face in the nervous bladed grass and go down into his own fuzziness and never open his eyes.

Chapter Fourteen

Each day in the office seemed more difficult than the last. They rarely spoke. Everything the older man did showed a certain calculation. Sometimes he would step over from the other side of the room to put a stack of papers on the boy's desk, and the boy would not look up but he could feel the sergeant standing there. He would stand there a moment too long, and then the papers would slap against the desk like a laugh.

But one day after a week of the restriction he came into the office and his manner was different. He slammed the screen door and tossed a wave at Swanson. As he sat at his desk he hummed and went brightly through his paper work, glancing up now and then to direct an amused smile at the boy. When the captain came in to sign papers Callan was loud, almost too friendly.

"Yes sir, Captain, just sign these few little things and we're all set. How's the badminton tourney coming, Captain? You're in charge of the post badminton tourney, aren't you? Yes, I thought so.

Good to see the men get a little sporting exercise, eh? And it's an important job too, organizing all that. You bet!"

Captain Loring smiled nervously and tried to look away, and then the sergeant reached out and slapped his back, chuckling as he watched the shoulders shrink in like a retreating shellfish. "Yes sir!" he boomed.

All morning he was like that, using himself, boisterous. And finally, leaning back in the chair with his hands folded over his stomach, he spoke to Swanson.

"How're you doing, kid?"

Swanson could not stop himself from looking up from the typewriter. But he did not answer.

"You getting along all right?" continued the sergeant. "Sometimes staying in all the time makes a man a little punchy. Myself, it don't bother me. But some fellows seem to get nervous if they can't get out and chase around every night."

"I'm all right."

"It's funny, though. If you get in the habit of running around, sometimes it takes years to get rid of. It's a shame being that way. If I had your youth and vitality I'd probably be directing it someplace. Staying in like this is a good start. I'd hate to see a nice healthy boy get on the wrong track at such an early age. It'd be a shame."

"Look, Sergeant Callan," said the boy. He felt steady as he watched the older man; a layer of coolness seemed to spread down through him. "I don't much care why you're talking this way, but

I think you'd do better if you saved it for somebody else."

For an instant the sergeant's face changed, darkened, but it recovered quickly and he went on in
the same amused tone. "Oh, so you think I'm being some particular way. Well, that's nice, isn't it?
If there's one thing I've always admired it's a
judge of human nature."

Swanson looked at him coolly.

"Yes, a judge of human nature is a very rare
thing. You don't often find them, not a good one.
Is that what you are Swanson? That's what you
think you are, anyway. Well let me tell you," he
said, the amusement vanishing from his voice, "you
don't know half as much as you think you know."

"I guess not," said Swanson. He felt something
happy and cruel working inside him.

"Not by a long shot you don't. You young guys
think you know the whole score, that's what gets
me about you guys." His face was flushed with beginning anger, and at the same time he seemed
surprised at the sudden turn of his own conversation.

The boy turned back to the typewriter.

"Listen Swanson, I told you once before I don't
like smart alecs." His lips quivered slightly and he
pushed them tight together as to gain control.

"What's wrong, Sergeant? I didn't think I said
anything that bad."

Callan's eyes grew wider and he leaned forward
over the desk, his mouth becoming grotesque as
it struggled with unspoken words. His hands

curled into fists and he stared without speaking. At last he turned away. He gazed at the wall and after several moments his breath released, slow and soundless. His whole frame seemed to collapse like a bellows. He pushed himself up from his chair and walked to the center of the room. His cheeks were still flushed but somehow his mood seemed different from anger. He put a hand to his tie and made a pitiful gesture at straightening the knot.

"I don't know why I get sore like that. I guess you think I'm kind of a hard-knocks character. A lot of the men think that, I suppose." He paused, staring out the window, and Swanson could not help watching him.

"I don't mean to ride you or string you along. Sometimes I just don't know how to act like I feel. Mostly I'm a soldier and that's the way I've always been and I guess there's a lot of things that I've never been able to learn how to do. I'm a soldier and that's about all. And that's what I've got to be if this company is going to amount to anything. Maybe you don't care about the company, but I do. I care because it's my job."

All the practiced quality was gone and as he gazed out the window he seemed stripped, naked. His eyes were glassy with hurt and his hands jerked slightly in the backwash of his speech. Swanson had never seen him so sincere, never heard him speak with such clearness or spontaneity. He felt a tinge of humiliation.

"I think I understand," he said.

"Yeah. Well, I don't know," the older man

muttered. He stood alone by the window and it was several minutes before he went back to his desk.

They started back to work in silence. Swanson could hear the ticking of the clock over the file cabinet. There was a new kind of quiet in the room. Once he turned to see the sergeant staring vacantly at his papers, not working, and again he was pierced with shame. He tried not to think of the man across from him, but he couldn't shake away his thoughts, and more than anything it was a kind of tenderness he felt. But how could he feel tenderness or sympathy for Callan? Only a few minutes before he had been supercilious, full of a biting superiority. He could think of the tightness of the past weeks and of Callan's behavior during that day and then it was easier to put these few minutes out of his mind.

It seemed a long time before the sergeant spoke again, a half hour perhaps. His voice drifted softly from across the room.

"Swanson."

"Yes?"

The sergeant was staring at a spot just above the screen door. He cleared his throat before going on. "How'd you like to go out for a beer after work?"

For almost a minute he didn't answer. The question caused a sick little flutter in his heart and he knew that despite its casualness it had been spoken with an effort. The sergeant was looking unconcerned at a spot over the screen door. But it had

been a great effort. Swanson knew it, and he knew
also that everything that had gone before, the
man's early-morning frivolity, his anger and its
turning . . . all of that had been part of the same
struggle. He felt hollowed out and he couldn't
keep an evenness to his voice when he answered.

"I don't much feel like it."

"You don't feel like it?"

"No."

Callan paused. He was not looking in the boy's
direction. "Okay," he said slowly. He turned back
to the papers on his desk and for a while there was
the rapid scratch of his pencil. Then, abruptly, he
got up and left the office.

There was a loneliness about the camp that only
the ready could see. It was like a wind that didn't
blow. It was a second air that hung in the streets.
It could creep inside, into the eyes of soldiers
walking silent at dusk on the wood of the wooden
sidewalks, or into a sudden burst of laughter or
the heartiness of a voice. It was with the men who
sat bent in the stalls of the latrines, their elbows
tucked into the warmth of their naked thighs, and
it was in the dryness of the concrete floor of the
shower room. It was in the bad gray smoke of a
forgotten cigarette. Or the holes burnt on table
edges, little moist grooves.

The loneliest couldn't write letters, for one had
to walk silent and careful in the second air.
Swanson tried to write letters but the effort stirred
the waiting pain and his head would slip back onto

his pillow while the white paper was like a crisp blanket across his chest, and if he slept the pencil dropped from his hanging hand to the floor.

He often sat numbly at the edge of his bunk, and as he sat there staring at the stove the three other men watched him. They were sensitive to things new and different, and instinctively they were considerate. They rarely addressed him. They tried to talk among themselves as though he weren't there. Sometimes the idle conversations would come to a halt, and in the frightening silence only Swanson would continue, his gaze fixed on the stove, his thoughts going on in the silence stronger than a spoken word, and the three other men would be aware of him, terribly. They could turn like Peeping Toms and watch him.

In those moments they felt an urge to speak, a compulsion. Aldous Brown tried one night.

"It's funny the way a place like this gets to a man. Specially you take someone smaaht. I'm not saying smaaht in the head, but someone who is smaaht all over. I mean someone who feels how things are. You put 'em in this here kind of place an I imagine they gonna go plumb crazy. It's bad enough for a dumb fella, but think how'd it be for a smaaht fella. Now it's tough, I'm sayin. But it ain't so bad that it can't be beat. Because you got a smaaht fella now, an he's gonna hate it more, but then because he's smaaht he's got more to beat it with."

He spoke out to the room, gently, philosophically, as though it were an unrelated thought. But when he'd finished the men waited and Tom Swanson lifted his head. His good-looking face took on a slow recognition, as if he'd caught it at the end and then thought back over it all. He looked about rather absently, at each of them. Then his face hardened and his eyes squinted and he turned and lay silent on his bunk.

Since that day of anger and asking, there had been a change in the office. Soldiers said that Callan was loosening up, that he had been drinking often in the enlisted men's club. But there was no loosening apparent to Swanson. Sometimes Callan came in with the rims of his eyes slightly red, but as always he was brusque, sharp, and as always the small room was choked and tense. He ran the company with the same ruthlessness. The captain came and went quickly, as if he were afraid.

But the change would begin to show itself in the late afternoon. As it grew toward the quitting hour the sergeant would leave his desk and move restlessly around the room. He would stand with his hands toward the stove, or gaze absently out the window. About his whole manner there was a vagueness. He would gaze out the window with his hands stuffed into his pockets, and his tight-muscled back, as it was silhouetted in the pale light from the window, seemed pitiful rather than strong. Facing away, he would begin to speak a little; he only made idle comments on the weather or work, yet over the bareness of the words there was something childish, a yearning.

Swanson would listen to the turned-away voice and he would be half sorry for the man, for now he knew perfectly what would come.

"I was wondering," the sergeant would say. "Maybe tonight you would like to go out for a beer? What d'yuh think?"

If not casually, it would come in another way.

"What the hell, Swanson! A beer or two's not gonna hurt yuh. C'mon, let's get the hell out of this office and grab ourselves a beer."

The boy's steady refusal did not prevent the scene from repeating itself on the next day, or the day after that. It had started, and now it was easier.

But strangely, there was no loss of dignity for the sergeant. He recovered from each refusal with a shrug of the shoulders or a sarcastic grunt. It was as if he could see himself as the scene was being enacted, and that was a security, as if he could never really be a fool if he saw his own actions.

Yet there was a deadly seriousness to it and Swanson knew it. Each time, when he answered, it was harder to maintain his calmness. Each time it was harder to leave the office and go to the hut and quiet the strain enough to sleep.

Chapter Fifteen

One night as the four hut mates sat in silence, there was a rap on the door. They looked up from the stove and glanced at one another. Nobody ever knocked. There was a moment of wondering, but before anyone could speak Swanson jumped up from his foot locker and went quickly to the door. He opened it and stepped outside so that they could not see. "What do you want?" Swanson said hoarsely. Callan was standing on the wooden sidewalk.

He was standing with the collar of his brown overcoat pulled up around his ears, and for a long moment they stared at each other. Swanson leaned back into the lighted hut. "It's for me," he said, shutting the door behind him.

Callan's hands were stuffed deep into the pockets of his overcoat, and he seemed to peek up at the boy. "Hiya," he said. It was a clumsy word for him and he tried to smile, and the thinness of the smile showed his soberness.

Swanson stood on the single step, his hand tight on the doorknob.

"Cold as hell," Callan went on. "November already."

"Is there some night work?" asked Swanson hurriedly.

"Oh, no. No. I thought I'd come by for a minute. I bought a car," he said.

Swanson looked down at the bundled figure. Callan glanced away, and the boy could see his nervousness and it was something to pity. He could see the tough lips quiver as they tried to smile. He took his hand from the doorknob and stepped down to the sergeant's level. He didn't want to be standing over him like that. "You bought a car?"

"Yeah," and he brightened. "An old forty-eight Hudson. Just bought it tonight from a sergeant over at the engineers." He hesitated and looked out to the gravel street. His cheeks were shiny red from the cold. "I thought maybe you'd like to take a look at it."

"You bought a car," he repeated dumbly. "Where's it parked?"

"Oh, out on the main lot."

The boy looked up and down the opposite row of huts, as though he were trying to get his bearings. He bit his lip. Despite everything he had prepared in himself, he could not stop the feeling that was inside him now. He had seen the sergeant standing below the door and he had been caught with something that was like the last warm instant before the flow of tears. It was a sympathy for the man that came out so quick and strong it almost shamed him. He had to turn away for a moment. "I guess we'd better see it," he said clearly. He took a step in the direction of the lot. "Shall we walk over?"

"Sure, sure." Callan scampered up alongside and as they walked down the wooden sidewalk the sergeant's bobbing head came no higher than his shoulder. They were both silent and Callan looked straight ahead.

At the lot he pointed toward the parked Hudson. "It's not much, huh?" There was a happy relief in his voice, as though he welcomed the chance to ridicule himself.

They went over to the car and Swanson inspected it seriously. "How much you pay?"

"Three hundred. I'm a sucker about cars. Always manage to pick up a lemon. This one runs pretty good, though."

Swanson circled the car, kicked the tires, and then stood back. There didn't seem to be anything else to do. His arms were close to his sides from the cold. "Oh, it's not so bad," he said.

"I guess not. It runs better'n it looks."

They stood without speaking, looking at the car. "Well," said Swanson.

"Maybe you should have brought a coat."

"Yeah, it's kind of cold." He turned as if to start back. "It's not such a bad deal, though. It'll be nice to have a car to get around in."

"Yeah," said Callan. He saw the boy's readiness to leave and he stuffed his hands deeper into his pockets, his head turning absently about the lot.

Swanson started slowly back and the sergeant walked beside him. "I just thought I'd show it to you." He laughed self-consciously.

"Well, it's not so bad."

"Say, have you ever gotten out into one of these little villages, besides Bernod that is? Bernod is just another Army town, but these other villages farther out?"

"I always wanted to, but I never got around to it. I guess I was in the habit of going straight to Bordeaux."

"You doing anything now? How'd you like to drive over to one of them, look around some?"

"What about the restriction?"

The sergeant looked away, embarrassed. "Ah hell, you with me it don't make any difference."

Inwardly Swanson laughed. Sarcastically. But still he didn't feel the old bitterness. As they walked along he asked himself how he could harbor hate toward a man like this. There was a childish quality about him, an open loneliness that was almost appealing. Maybe it would be good to go on out with him. If he could be at ease with the man it would be like getting things straight with himself. Maybe he'd only been making it hard for himself.

They reached the hut and Swanson was pleased with his own calmness. He felt clear. "Sure, I'd like to take a ride. See how the old Hudson goes."

The brightness on the sergeant's face was almost surprise.

"If you wait I'll get a coat," said Swanson. He went into the hut and took his coat from the locker. He went back outside with only a haphazard wave at his startled hut mates.

The sergeant drove slowly, his large hands fixed on the wheel with a peculiar solidness. It was not a difficult road but he drove with a certain perched-forward intensity, as if to avoid conversation.

After fifteen or twenty kilometers they reached a little village that the road map showed was Lebec. It was a village of perhaps a dozen stone houses, all lining the road, and Callan stopped the Hudson in front of the best lighted of the houses and they could see that it was a little country bar.

"You want to go in?" he asked.

Swanson laughed.

"You want to?" he asked again.

"All right," he said. "Why not?"

They climbed out of the car and went into the nearly empty bar. There were several round tables against the back wall, and at one of them two men played chess. Behind the small zinc bar an elderly woman sat on a stool and knitted. The sergeant hesitated, then approached her with three fingers raised and said, "Cognac."

He took the three cognacs she poured and brought them to an empty table, drinking one of them quickly before either of them had sat down.

They settled themselves into the wooden chairs and for a while they did nothing but glance around the barren room. The sergeant pushed one of the remaining cognacs toward Swanson and tried again to smile. "Good medicine against the cold," he said.

"Sure is," said Swanson, wanting somehow to help him. He sipped out of the little glass.

"I've never been much of a conversationalist," Callan said. "I guess that's one art I've never gotten around to developing."

"It's not so important anyhow."

"No? I thought maybe you were one of these guys who hold stake by conversation. You like the French and I hear they're famous for it."

"Well, when I say it's not important I mean it isn't essential. But when it's good talk it's just something happy to do, like a dividend."

"Yeah? How?"

"Maybe I can't even explain it," he said.

"You think I wouldn't understand?"

Swanson looked at him to be sure there was no sarcasm in his question, and there was not. He seemed too nervous for sarcasm.

"What about that girl in Bordeaux?" continued Callan. "What kind of talks do you have with her?"

"Jesus, Sergeant." And despite the man's apparent innocence, he couldn't continue to match it. He shook his head and drank the rest of his drink. "It's been quite a time now since I've been able to see her to talk to."

"Oh . . . yeah." He fumbled with the two

empty glasses in front of him, glancing around the room. Then he got up and went back to the bar and ordered more cognac. He took a long time counting over the change with the woman and when he came back to the table he cleared his voice roughly before he sat down.

"Listen, Swanson, about that restriction. I don't think I'm gonna keep you on it much longer." He did not look at the boy as he spoke and he cleared his voice once more. "You're pretty well squared away, it seems to me, and I don't see why you shouldn't be able to go into town now that you've got all the office work down pat. In a day or two I'll have that pass of yours back in the box." He turned almost shyly toward the boy. "I guess you'd like that." He made a thin little laugh.

"I'd like it fine."

"Well then, why not? I don't do anything against you on purpose."

Swanson checked an impulse to thank him. He watched the fresh glass of cognac in front of him, not knowing whether he would drink it or not. Neither of them spoke for several minutes.

"I don't speak this French like you do," Callan began again. "But just the same I know this country pretty well. I had my share of it during the war, you know. Germany too."

"Yes, you told me one night."

"Told you? Oh that. About being a hero," he mumbled.

He seemed to reflect over those moments, and then he drank from his glass as if it were all too distant to be remembered. But when he set down his glass he brought out his wallet and unfolded a worn sheet of parchment. "The French government gave me the Croix de Guerre," he said, spreading it on the table. "This is the certificate."

It struck Swanson that he was not showing it in a boastful way, but more as though it were a wayward fact that had crossed his mind. More as if it were a bubble out of his new innocence. And the man's innocence was almost disturbing. He could brace himself against the cold superiority, the practiced sarcasm, but now when the man was stripped and nervous he felt stripped himself. It almost hurt to see him in such a state, fumbling and awkward with the rigidness of sincerity. He couldn't be graceful with it. Abrupt rather. Abrupt and hurting, the way he took out his medals without being boastful about it.

Swanson turned the certificate around and glanced over it politely. At the bottom he saw the signature of General de Gaulle.

"They were pretty loose with those," Callan broke in. "But I got that one along with the DSC." He took the certificate back and glanced over it as though it were new to him. He folded it up again and he had the appearance of being light and jolly as he stuffed the wallet into his rear pocket. "About all it's good for is a free drink once in a while." He chuckled, trying to make a joke of it.

Swanson found himself watching the other man. He couldn't help it. He had never been able to

before, not with the tension, but he knew he could
watch and listen now and he did so with strange,
sudden eagerness. "What did you do after the
war?" he asked.

"Oh, Germany awhile. Then back to the States,
you know, one camp to another." With a wave of
his hand he made a "you know" gesture.

"Have you ever been married, Sergeant Callan?"

"Married?" he said, startled. "Have I been married? Why do you ask?" But then he went ahead
without waiting for an answer, his fingers tapping
all the while on the table top. "Yeah, sure I was.
Still am, for all I know, unless she divorced me
somewhere along the line. But I haven't heard
about it if she has." He laughed to himself, as
though something in the memory was amusing.
"Betty Lou was her first name and goddamn if I
can remember now what her last name was. Met
her on my first leave after I got back, June of forty-
six. Providence, Rhode Island, that's where it was,
in Ellie's Bar on Seventh Street." He leaned back
in his chair as though to give himself time to re-
construct it all. "I'd been drinking in there two
or three days and it seemed like every time I
turned around she'd be sitting there on the stool
next to me. Maybe I was buyin her drinks, I don't
know. Betty Lou," he mused. "I never been so
drunk in my life as those thirty days. They all knew
me in that bar, and then one afternoon that
woman and I went out an got married. . . . Jesus
Christ . . . I still can't figure it. We went out
an got married an when we came back they gave

us the run of the bar for free . . . Jesus, three, four days. That woman, Betty Lou, she had a little cabin out in back of her mother's place and I stayed in it with her the whole thirty days. Christ! To tell yuh the truth, I don't think I screwed her more than twice."

He leaned forward toward Swanson, suddenly more serious. "She had a bad cavity right between her front teeth. When she smiled you could see it." He paused, and then, as if it were all ludicrous, he laughed, roughly. "She was no spring chicken, that's what I'm tryin to say, an ugly bitch. And I damn well got out of there when my leave was up."

Once again he leaned back in his chair and his fingers resumed their tapping on the table top. Apparently he was disappointed with what he had related.

"Listen, Swanson, I've had plenty of women, all over. The thing is, don't get involved with 'em, give 'em a lay or maybe two and let it go at that. Boom bam thankyou ma'am, it's the only way. These guys that get all wound up with a woman!" He grunted. "It takes something soft to get like that."

He had become a little aggressive with the flow of his own talk, yet at the same time he seemed displeased. He drank off his cognac and went quickly to the bar and brought back two more. He put one in front of Swanson and he put his hand over the face of his own. He stared over at the two men playing chess. He stared at their quietness.

"Look," he said more softly. "Maybe that's one reason why I cut off your passes. I don't want to see you get all hung up with some woman, especially a frog dame who you'd probably be ashamed to be seen with in the States. It happens all the time over here, it's an old story. I'm a few years older than you and I got a little experience behind me, and maybe I'm just trying to help you out."

Somehow, Swanson did not resent it. He was curious to hear more. To have the man unfolding before him seemed almost a phenomenon, and if advice had to be part of it, what difference? Advice was easy enough to put off. What he wanted was to hear him talk, just hear him talk. He nodded, trying to urge him on.

But across the table, the sergeant remained silent. He fingered the hard knot of his OD tie and then the fingers crept up to play with the loose red skin of his neck. As he had begun to speak of his marriage in Providence, he had become rather excited, and the earlier humility had slipped away in the excitement and now he fingered his neck, pinching it as though to calm himself. "How'd you like the way the Hudson went?" he said finally.

"Fine," said Swanson, disappointed.

"Well, you gotta figure you're taking a chance when you get an old car like that. I guess it's not such a bad deal, though."

"What made you decide to get a car?"

"Oh, it's good to get out of the camp now and then. You know how it is. In my job I can't be

staying around after hours and mixing with the
men, but then again, a man can't help wanting
a drink or two every once in a while and a car
solves it."

"I guess it's a lonely job, huh?" asked Swanson.
He leaned his elbows forward on the table.

The sergeant didn't answer. He shrugged his
shoulders and took out a cigarette and lighted it.
"Say. I been meaning to ask you. Where'd you
learn to pass the football like that?"

The question distracted the boy. He wanted to
hear Callan speak more about himself. "I played
in high school," he said.

"Quarterback?"

He nodded.

"You're kinda tall for a quarterback. How tall
are you, Swanson?"

"Oh, six one."

"Six one! I thought you were taller than that.
You got the appearance of being taller. But you're
not skinny either. Just about how a guy should
be."

Swanson laughed, but then he spoke up as if
he'd remembered something. "I used to be pretty
thin, my sophomore, junior years. Those linemen
really liked to take their shots at me."

"Well, I imagine you wouldn't a been playin
ball if you couldn't take it."

The boy took a sip from his cognac.

"Yeah, I could tell it even before I saw you out
on the ball field, that you were an athalete. But
what makes it better is that you got it up in the

head too. One without the other ain't much good.
I guess you'll be going to college when you get
out, huh?"

"Yeah, I think so."

"Good. Maybe if I coulda done it all over I
woulda gone to college. But it don't matter about
me, you're the important thing now. Get in there
and get that education. You got the head for it
an maybe I never had."

"Nah . . . sure you do. . . . And hell, it
doesn't take much to get through college."

"Gettin through college? You bet it does. Oh,
they're some guys come out graduates that I
wouldn't piss on the best part of, but just the same
you gotta hand it to anyone who kept at it long
enough to make it."

"Yeah, maybe so." The boy smiled. "I'm always
hearing you call the college guys in the company
punks."

"Yeah, well." He shook his head. "I guess maybe
I'm just jealous, is all."

His saying that made Swanson self-conscious.
And for a moment he couldn't help liking the man
across from him. To try to ply him with questions
seemed almost disrespectful. He turned away so that
he would not have to watch him, and then presently
Callan was speaking again, in the slow humble way
of earlier in the evening, and the boy was light and
easy as he listened. They talked of small things, of
cars and of how they would like to watch a good college football game. When Callan spoke of himself, it
was often with good-natured ridicule, and each

time Swanson was surprised, even pleased. They drank a cognac or two more, and Swanson found himself talking too, about nothing of great importance, yet things that interested him as he spoke, his boat trip to the European theater, his five-day leave to Spain, and all the while the sergeant listened with eyes gently bright and interested.

When they got up to leave the two Frenchmen in the corner looked up from their chessboard and called "Bon soir." They both turned and waved and as they got outside in the car and started toward the camp Swanson opened his window and felt the good night air and its closeness.

As they came into the camp and toward the company street the sergeant pulled the car over to the side. "Well, Swans, I'm gonna put the car over in the lot so I'll dump you here."

"Right," he said. He got out and looked at the sergeant behind the wheel. Callan made a half salute, half wave, smiling, and the boy returned it.

As he went toward the hut he thought of all the cognac they had had and how they were not drunk. He whistled a tune that had been popular before he left the States. I bet Callan feels pretty good, he mused. He laughed to himself. And why not? I feel kind of good myself, he thought.

Chapter Sixteen

The boy was up early, before reveille, and he went down to the shower hut to shave while the water was still hot. When he thought of the night before he couldn't help feeling a certain relief. It had been without strain, almost pleasant. And his pass, he would be having the pass back.

As he was shaving he heard the first buzz of the camp loudspeaker and then the worn record of reveille, and he was glad he was up early, glad of the morning.

He came into the office and the sergeant was already at his desk. "Morning, Sergeant."

"Morning, Swanson." The sergeant did not lift his head from his work, but though it was a distant greeting it did not have the coldness of other days. The boy began his work and later, when Callan was inspecting the huts, he looked through the pass box. His pass had been returned. The lightness increased. It was almost an excitement.

In the afternoon Callan spoke to him. "See your pass in the box?"

The boy hesitated. "Yes, I did," he admitted.

"I put it back this morning. You're off restriction now, Swanson."

He nodded a kind of thanks and neither of them spoke again until late in the afternoon, until nearly quitting time.

"Swanson."

"Yeah?"

"Ready for a beer?"

Swanson was standing at the file cabinet and he closed the big steel door slowly. He heard the sergeant and all the pleasure of the day seemed suddenly false, precarious. "I don't think so," he said. "Not tonight."

There was a silence. The boy kept himself near the file cabinet.

"Sure?"

"Yeah, not tonight."

He went back to his desk and already he could feel the shadow that would hang into his evening, his evening in Bordeaux, his evening with Solange. The discouragement was a heaviness all through him. Why does he have to push it? he thought. The man was pacing rigidly about the office and he couldn't help watching him. And so he was hurt. Or was it anger? And as the boy watched him he could feel his will sliding. He didn't want the man to be hurt. And it seemed suddenly very important that he know Callan, important that he should be at ease around him, important that there never again be that strain. If I could sit for

one night, he thought, just sit and talk with him.
If that strain could get finished forever!

And the sergeant stopped his pacing and turned
toward him. He was trying to smile and in his
smile was that same thinness, the same quiver as
when he had come sober to the hut the night before. "Look Swans, you've got your pass now. Do
what you want. I just thought we could go out and
have a coupla beers and talk some. The work's pil-
ing up in here and I won't have the chance in a
few days and so I thought we just might have a
coupla short ones tonight."

It was true, thought Swanson quickly, he didn't
have to go, he had his pass and there was no pres-
sure. How long had he waited now to take that
pass? Couldn't he wait another night? He looked
at the man and it was hurting to see him like that,
awkward, tentative.

"Okay," he said suddenly. "Hell, why not?"

But it was not only that night that they went
out to the country bars, but the following night
and the night after. Each time the boy was reluctant and yet he went, and he went with a driving
desire to speak some final truth, a truth that would
end forever the waiting tension. And yet he never
could. He struggled in himself for words, and they
seemed always false or insufficient, and it was as if
he must know the very heart of the man.

They drank. The old Hudson sped over the country roads and they stopped in each wayside vil-

lage and drank. The evenings began in a cold and
distracted way. The drives out along the small dirt
roads were empty and strained, and the only fiber
between them was the motion of the road as it un-
curled beneath the slow orange lights. And when
they found their bar Callan would remain for a
long time away from the table, wandering about
with a cognac or beer in his hand. In nearly all
the bars there were one or two miniature pool
tables and he sauntered around them, restless, and
he would play with the little red balls, rolling
them listlessly down to the end of the table. After
a while he would sit down and they would drink
in silence.

The man's nervousness infected the boy. He
wanted to speak and he couldn't bring himself to
it. And then at some point he was no longer waiting to speak, but he was listening, listening
through the rose of drunkenness to the close and
heavy voice.

"Just sixteen I was when I first came in. Those
were the days, Swanson, hard days but good ones.
They used to put the privates in the stables. Eight
or ten of us would be in there but the others
would be playing craps or just screwin around and
they wouldn't do nothin until they seen an officer comin. Then they'd all jump up and start
workin. The officer would come in and look around.
In those days the officers were men an you could
respect them. And the officer would come in and
look around and it would be me he'd come up to.

Cause he knew. He knew I'd been workin right along. He'd say somethin, 'Good boy, Callan,' or somethin like that.

"Maybe I wasn't so social but I always knew how to work. I was the youngest sergeant in the regiment an when they first put me up for sergeant some battalion major started talkin around that I was too young for it. So they took me up to the colonel of the regiment. He knew me, he knew who I was. 'There's some talk about you being too young for sergeant,' he said. And then he didn't say anything for a while. He just looked at me and I looked at him. 'But I don't think so,' he said. 'I think you're going to do just fine.' "

Callan paused in his narrative, thinking back on what he had related.

"And those were times," he said slowly.

For three nights they drove out in the old Hudson and on the fourth day Callan left the Orderly room early, before the quitting time. As the boy cleared his desk he suddenly felt his own tiredness. It was a tiredness that ached through his body and made his chest heavy. He walked back to the empty hut and undressed slowly and lay on his cot. He was glad he was alone. Somehow he felt sheepish in the hut, almost a stranger to it.

Sam came through the door and sat on the bunk across and began to unlace his boots. As he unlaced the boots he looked over at the boy. "Say, you been drinking with Callan?"

"What do you mean? When?"

"Last coupla nights. Someone from over at Engineers was tryin to tell me they seen you two out drinkin."

The boy shifted his position on the bunk. "Yeah," he said. "I've had a few drinks with him."

"What! Yeah? Say, you don't wanna be doin that. You don't wanna be runnin around with that guy."

"Why not?"

"Why not! Je-sus, man. You oughta know what kind of guy he is."

"What?" he said quickly. "What kind of guy?"

"Je-sus. A goddamn sonofabitch, that's what. A goddamn rotten dirty sonofabitch."

The boy looked at Sam and then away.

"What the hell, you don't do yourself no good foolin around with a guy like that."

"Okay. All right. Goddammit, why can't you just let me lie here and sleep?"

He turned himself toward the wall. The tiredness was all through him but it was a long time before he could sleep. He could think of Sam on the other bunk and he could think of the sergeant and the three nights of drinking. Why had he gone? But then why not, too? There was nothing wrong in talking to Callan. Maybe it was even good, it could help a lot of things, it could ease a lot of things. He thought of the way the man had been, innocent, trying to talk. It was almost a sympathy he felt for him. And yet there were times too when he felt a real respect. There was a force about the man. The way he talked, the heavy

voice and the hunch of the shoulder as he lit on
something and spoke with sureness. And he was a
man capable of understanding. He had seen it in
him many times, seen it in the choice of a word
or a smile at the right time. And it was the kind
of understanding that came out of a certain rigidness, a rigidness that made it seem stronger.

The boy twisted on his bunk. Callan's all right,
he thought, and at the same time he could remember all the past weeks, their tension, and he could
remember all that he thought he knew. But he
pushed it down quickly in his mind. No, Callan's
all right. Besides, it doesn't matter, he thought.
Tomorrow he would go into Bordeaux to see
Solange and so this didn't matter. He would be
going into town. He turned in his bed and tried
to think of nothing but Bordeaux and the girl.

Chapter Seventeen

But he did not go into Bordeaux on the following night, nor did he go for a long time to come. He spent his evenings drinking with Callan. Each time he swore it was the last, and he went each time with a pulling reluctance. And yet he went. He went in a plunging way, as if he could throw himself into the heart of it, as if the heart of it would solve the endless weeks of outside struggle.

And too, there was something about the man that seemed rare and understanding. The boy often found himself talking, fired by the man's audience, talking as he never had before. Callan seemed to know, to understand exactly, even before a thing was fully said. He was able to anticipate and that spurred the boy on until he was speaking of things long forgotten, a distant conversation, a scene from his boyhood, and he spoke as if to live over and know the essence of each memory, for the man spurred him on and seemed to understand.

But it was not an easy or natural communication. It came only after the evening's early tenseness, after heartless rides through Pessac, Montendre, Blaye, Barsac, after many drinks and long, tight silences. But almost inevitably it came. At some point it would be suddenly there, brought on by something very slight, a word or two, a gesture of the hand that came easily. Something sparked it and then would come the rush of hot live drunkenness that was more than drink, an awareness, a living thing that jumped and danced between them.

"Listen, Sergeant!" and the boy would point to a nearby table of Frenchmen, his voice already excited. "Look at those men there, those peasants. Look at the way they sit, the way they hold their glasses, the way they laugh or talk. You look at them and you seem to know them, their whole lives. Even the smallest gesture . . . everything they do seems to represent them, even sum them up. It's because they're solid. Solid in their own world. Solid without ever having to think about it. No, listen, in their own way they're like gems, they're filled up right to the brim, and it's because they don't have to think about what they are or who they are, they don't have to let themselves get torn apart by thinking of it."

"Sure. Sure, I know what you mean."

"Maybe that's what's good about country people. They give themselves time, their thinking is something that creeps up on them, they don't have to force it. Look, maybe I'm not saying this right."

"Sure you are!"

"No, look, it's like this. You see so many guys that are trying so hard they lose themselves. They're trying to know who they are. They read, for instance, but they don't read with real under-standing, I mean real, deep understanding, the kind that goes all through you like electricity. But they read anyhow, and they try to be learned that way, they try to adapt what they've read or what people say is right, they try and paste it onto themselves like it'll help them know who they are. But it can't be done that way!"

"Kid, I know what you're driving at, I do!"

"No, it can't be done that way. Everything good has to start from the inside and then spread out. And everybody's trying to do it the other way!"

"Sure, sure," said the sergeant, nodding him along. His face, poked forward, was a redness of understanding, and it glistened with a readiness to absorb.

"That's why I like these people here." The boy's arm swept out to indicate the group across the room, the country Frenchmen as they drank and laughed. "They are! They don't have to kill them-selves trying. They are! And maybe you'll say but Christ they're not much, but still they're whole and that's more than some sharp people, some real intelligent people who can't match their intelli-gence in their hearts and so they're just left kind of dangling in mid-air. And it's the same way with goodness and virtue," said the boy, sweeping on. "So much goodness is up there dangling in mid-air. A lot of people are good, but they're only good because it's something they've learned or because the environment is just right for it. And then put them somewhere else, put them in the muck, and the whole thing collapses. They haven't got any real foundation for their goodness. It's all that adapted stuff. And it's going to collapse because it isn't inside out! It's got to be inside out, that's the thing!"

The boy would talk on and between them would be their four fists tight with knowing. Everything going forward, upward. Everything important because one of them was saying it. The boy spoke as he never had before. His mind seemed to rip open and come alive to fragments, unexpressed and fleeting knowledge that he caught and threw into the heat of the ready eyes facing him, eyes he no longer feared. He challenged them with the force of himself, his pushing, drunken sureness. He spoke anything that tore through his mind, quick perceptions that seemed fantastic and glorious in their reach, a torrent of words coming like an over-flow to the tightness of the evening's start.

"That's it, boy," urged the older man. "You're sayin things now, just keep goin, keep goin like that!" The sergeant would stand in his excitement, slapping his hand down on the table in a burst of agreement. "Goddamn kid, I'm listenin to you, I know what you mean, I know what you mean all right. Jesus! Two men out of nowhere! We understand things. You understand. I understand! Jesus!"

The boy did not know when it was that Callan lost his innocence. But it went. It went sly and unnoticed as the intensity of their times together grew. There was no more hesitancy or self-ridicule. There was only Callan, aggressive, certain, Callan with tight fists on the table and a heaviness in his hunched-forward shoulders as he talked from a directly opposite nearness.

And in each night there would always be a time when he would begin to dominate their talks. His voice would drop into a strange control, a quick control that seemed to make a lie out of his earlier excitement.

"It's the survival of the fittest, boy, and I believe that. If you're fit you know you're fit and you don't waste no time with the others and their weaknesses. You run through 'em, Swans, because you gotta. You gotta keep moving and if you have a friend it's got to be a friend that's moving too, the same way you are, the same direction. Me, I don't make many friends because sure as hell, one time or another they're gonna hold you back. You, you're different. You got the strength that it takes. Hell yes. Look at you then look at someone else. Look at Captain Loring for instance an you can see the difference. He's as weak as they come. He's weak but mind you he ain't dumb. And it's weakness that gives him eyes. A guy like him can sit and watch himself go down. If he was doing his

job, if he was tryin to be a man, it would probably be worse because then he couldn't see anything. I guess he knows it, too," said the voice,
sneaky, happy. "I could put him under my thumb
and squeeze him dead like a bug. He's scared of me,
Swanson. He knows a little bit about what he's
doing. He can feel not to screw with me."

More stimulated than ever, the boy would try
to break in with an excited objection. But it was
the sergeant now and his voice would increase its
careful loudness while a raised hand motioned for
quiet. "No, no, boy, just you wait a minute while
the old sergeant says something."

Anxiously he would wait and listen, and inevitably his own urge to speak faded. He would drink
and listen.

"See, the whole damn world's unconscious, and
when you know what you're doing you can tear
through it. And I know what I'm doing. Listen,
boy, there may be some things I can't say well,
but that doesn't mean that I don't know them.
There's things inside me"—and his hand would
jerk toward his chest—"there's things there that
I can't express good. But that don't mean that I
don't know. I know just as well as if I could speak
it. And even better."

Sometimes, as if words were not enough, Callan
would cease talking and leap crazily into a silence.
His hands would open and close like a pulse, as if
he were writhing in his own-made heat. His hands
would open and close and his eyes would move
over the room, demanding, pushing. His shoulders

closed into his neck and his eyes would swarm over the room as in a desire to smash it, all of it, with his hands.

At the company the soldiers were talking of the two of them and their nights of drinking. He knew it by the way glances found him and then turned resentfully away. Or by the sudden silence when he entered the recreation room, worse because he anticipated it. Many times he saw that men were about to speak. They would be casual as they confronted him, yet cautious, and they would begin in a light manner that he knew was prepared, for the lightness would vanish when they got ready to come out with it. They would stammer, looking away as if they had been distracted.

"What is it? What do you want to say?" he challenged.

Sergeant Clyde came and sat on the Orderly room steps during the noon hour one day. Swanson went out and sat beside his old depot sergeant and for a while they smoked and talked about Clyde's wife and how she liked living in a French farmhouse.

"Sure she likes it," Clyde said. "She makes every place home, that woman. If she knows she gonna be someplace more'n ten minutes she does some little thing or another and right away it's home." He flipped his cigarette out onto the gravel street. He watched it burn for a moment. "Maybe I shouldn't done that," he observed, gesturing behind him toward the Orderly room. "The man'll have me in jail." He turned abruptly toward Swanson, smiling. "You miss the old depot? You miss that frog crew of yours?"

Swanson chuckled. "Yeah, I guess I do."

Clyde moved his head and peered closer at the boy. "Old red-eyes," he said. "What's you been doing, drinking all the wine in France?"

"What?" said Swanson, embarrassed.

"I heard you and him been drinking up a storm."

Swanson didn't answer, and the sergeant spit down between his legs, a pause. "I reckon it's nobody's business what you do, son." He stood up and tucked his fatigue shirt down into his pants, and as he did so he looked through the window into the Orderly room. "Come on out some night," he said, "and have dinner with me and the wife. She'll cook up something nice and fancy for you."

As he walked off toward the Mess Hall, Swanson sat on the steps and he was empty and sad.

In his own hut he was beginning to feel a stranger. He was there only occasionally now, and when he was there he sensed their attitude toward him had stiffened. He sensed it with a deep, resentful anger.

One night the quiet of the hut was broken by Sam, who burst through the door and paused rigidly when he saw the boy.

"You know what the sonofabitch did? You know what he did today, dontcha Swanson?"

He looked up from his bunk. "What are you talking about, Sam?"

"Callan. You know damn well what I'm talking about. He musta given you them papers to type up."

Swanson regarded the other man steadily. "I typed up some court-martial papers on Berhl. Is that what you mean?"

"Damn rights that's what I mean." He shook his fist in defense of Berhl, who was the mail clerk, fat and lazy, one of his only friends. "He don't have to court-martial him for that. Two hours late on a pass! You think that's enough reason to court-martial a man!"

"Don't ask me," he said steadily.

"You're damn rights I'm asking you," he went on. He was without caution in his anger. "It's funny to even see you around here in the first place, and I guess you'd be the one to ask, all right."

Swanson jumped up. "What do you mean?"

Sam hovered by the door. Aldous Brown and Pop watched from their foot lockers.

"I asked you what you meant," repeated Swanson tightly. And as he leaned toward the other man he could anticipate the response. He could read the unspoken words on his lips. You're Callan's big buddy, ain't you? It would be something like that, or maybe worse, and he waited for it.

But Sam did not answer. The red drained from his face and he went and sat down on his bunk.

"What the hell you think you're doing," demanded Swanson, "talking to me like that?"

"I didn't mean nothin. I was just hot."

"You damn well better not mean anything." He stared down at the seated subdued figure.

I don't give a damn about this guy, he thought rapidly. I don't give a damn about him or Berhl or anybody else. None of them, he told himself, conscious of the others in the room. He knew what they were thinking. They were accusing him, all of them, sore because they thought he was close with Callan. Well, goddammit, they better not try to tell him anything. He wouldn't have it.

For a moment he considered leaving the hut and going to the club, anywhere. But he checked himself. He had stayed in to get some sleep and that's what he was going to do. He sat down on his bunk and kicked off his unlaced boots. As he sat stocking-footed on the bunk his own tiredness flooded over him. He could feel the sharpness of his nerves. He could feel Aldous Brown and Pop watching him, and he knew that it wasn't in accusation.

Christ, didn't they realize that he had his own feelings? Didn't they know that he felt the thing too? The mornings, did they have any idea of the heaviness of the mornings, how it was to wake up with guilt so damned black and heavy he would only want to sink back into sleep? How it was to get out of bed and go through the business of

dressing, while all the time his head pressed and
throbbed in shame? No, dammit, nobody was going to accuse him. He could do that for himself.
It was part of each waking, that searching back
over the night before, trying to draw up the root
of his shame, trying to find what it was that carried so darkly through the night to spring alive
into that pulling morning torment. He could never
touch on any single word or deed that might have
started it. The shame was fluid, dark, running from
the whole of the evening, an overtone. He couldn't
shake it or put it aside. He could only make reso-
lutions, each morning a resolution, fierce, fixed,
angry. No more drinking. No more wild red evenings of crazy foundationless talk. . . . It was the
only way he could begin the day. He would go into
the office and labor through the mechanics of his
work, but then as the daylight hours passed his
anger would become thin, meaningless. He would
be weary and dull. He told himself that it was
boredom he felt, and when Callan asked him if he
was ready for a beer, he would go.

Even Captain Loring saw fit to comment. "You
gentlemen certainly look bedraggled," he said,
peering over the stack of papers he was signing.
He spoke in a tentative, half-joking way. Nothing in their appearance was "bedraggled" and
they both looked up and waited for him to go on.
He laughed thinly, twisting a pencil in his nervous fingers. "Been doing a little drinking, eh?"
Swanson could see it was an effort for the man.

It was obvious he was attempting some sort of reprimand and that already it had become too much
for him. Once again the captain laughed, and it
was sad, embarrassing.

"I drink now and then," said the sergeant from
his desk, loudly, "and I imagine Private Swanson
does too. Why do you ask, Captain?"

"Oh . . . well . . ." He shuffled the stack of
papers in front of him, set down his pencil, then
quickly picked it up again.

"What's on your mind, Captain, is something
wrong with the work in here?"

"The work? Why, no. No, Sergeant Callan, certainly not. Why the work is excellent, very good."

Sergeant Callan stood up and crossed the room
to Swanson's desk where the captain was sitting in
a pulled-up chair. He sat on a corner of the desk
looking down at the officer.

"What is it then? Did you want to say something about drinking?"

"Oh, not really. I'm certainly in favor of a
drink now and then, if it's not in excess."

"Is that right? Is that what you wanted to say,
Captain?"

"Why, I suppose. I didn't have anything particular in mind." He looked over at the door and
chuckled.

The sergeant continued to stare down at the
man, whose eyes dropped back to the stack of papers. Finally, as Callan remained sitting on the
desk, the captain once more put aside his pencil.
"I guess I can sign the rest of these this after-

noon." He stood up and looked pleadingly at Swanson. "That'll be time enough won't it, Swanson?"

"Yes sir," he answered quietly.

"Well, I'll be in this afternoon, eh?" He glanced about the office as if he had awakened in a strange room, and then he seemed to find himself, for he went quickly to the door and out into the street.

Callan remained for a moment longer at the desk, but he did not speak or look at Swanson. It was still early, and his coldness, his rigid manner during that part of the day had not changed. He seemed quite alone as he stared out after the retreating figure of the captain. It was not until late afternoon that he mentioned it. It was when he was beginning to put his work aside, his movements restless as they always were then. "That Loring," he said disgustedly. He shook his head so that the boy could see. "That's something, isn't it? Christ Almighty." He snorted, as if they were ridiculing him together.

Chapter Eighteen

There was hardly a night when they weren't driving over the country roads, stiff and quiet during the early ride, loud and reckless on the return. There were few nights when some village bar didn't stiffen to their challenging, foreign presence.

"A couple of warriors!" the sergeant would shout in English. Drunkenly, he would shout it like a discovery. "That's what we are, Swanson, a couple of warriors!"

The boy often protested against another evening. He was tired, nervous, uncertain, and in the dread gray of afternoon the protest bunched inside him until it spurted painful like a plea. Invariably the sergeant was offended. He would respond in quick, personal anger, as if he were being turned on, and the protest, in the boy's tiredness, would shatter and die.

And always, at some point in the evening, he would come alive again, responding to the drinks and the intense presence of the older man. Once more the world was vivid, heated, and his uncertain tiredness would seem a weak thing of the past. It was this he lived for, this warm moment choked with astounding perceptions and a man opposite who could understand. Suddenly he could see the world and that was the excitement, and with it all was a frenzied thankfulness for the man across, for it was his understanding that capped the glory of those moments.

He could see the world through a thousand depths and angles, the four wooden walls springing alive to his nakedness, breathing, strutting, bowing like charm to a stranger. All of it would salute his brand-new eyes. All of it. Unknowingly, the people leaped into another realm. Peasants became faces under the false light, faces with skin like hide, or they were denim jackets gracing dry, humped bodies, or leathered voices rising, falling —voices with a sameness that moved quick toward death; they were many things while she watched, the soft-bearded proprietress, watching while her black blouse was full of breasts to the navel and her legs coiled the stool like splitting sacks, watching, wheezing, watching with the blind eyes of time.

Not piece by piece did he see it, for then it was nothing. Only when it came at once, together, only then did he feel the excitement and he could extend his hand, offer it slow and curious as one about to touch, extend his hand and sum it all with a few drugged words. He could make that summation, or so it seemed, for the man across would cry as in release, "That's it, that's it perfectly, Tom, I see it, I see it!"

It was almost too much, this communion, this sharing, and for a moment they would lapse into heavy wonder and when that had eased the sergeant would speak. "It's amazing . . . the way you can point to the heart of a thing . . . because nothing's any good unless you can go to the heart . . . and you got that ability. . . . You can do it, boy. . . . You got that ability and you got guts too . . . not something flighty. . . . It's with guts and that's what makes it good . . . those two things together."

Night after night the Hudson rolled out of the parking lot into the undiscovered countryside. Bussac, Graves, Medoc, Libourne. All the villages within driving distance saw them once or more. At times the boy felt trapped in a great drawing force outside himself. Dreams ripped at his drunken sleep, dreams of himself perched on a huge belt that moved steadily into a darkness ahead as he grasped at the passing walls. "Can't we stay around at the club?" he sometimes pleaded.

"That place! Why do yuh want to waste your time with those guys? Those gutless bastards!"

The sergeant spoke often of guts, the need to have guts. His own capacity seemed unending, for drink, for frenzied talk, and his driving force seemed to gather strength with each passing hour

of the night. "Guts! Guts!" he sometimes shouted.
"Christ if I don't hate weakness!"

He hated weakness and he saw it everywhere.
He would draw back disdainfully at the sight of
it—the sight of a run-down farmhouse, a beggar, a
whore old before her time. One night they sat and
watched a young Frenchman among a crowd of
peasants at the next table, and the Frenchman was
not a peasant like the others, a clerk rather, or
perhaps a student, for his voice was clearer and
with an accent learned from the cities. He laughed
as he spoke, and his cheeks colored to the pleasure
of what he was saying, and his hands moved in
rapid gestures that seemed strange against the na-
tures of the others. The sergeant watched him
silently, coolly, and he heard the young man break
into high laughter. He turned toward Swanson, his
expression slow and disgusted. "Shit!" he said.

He saw weakness all about him. In the late
hours peasants dropped unconscious over lonely
wooden tables, and in passing by invariably he
would touch them, as by mistake, push them with
an elbow or a leg. "They oughta put those guys in
the gutters," he snorted. "If there's one thing I
hate it's a man who can't hold his liquor."

But he never saw it as a weakness in Swanson,
for as the nights continued the moments of excitement became less frequent for the boy and he
would be drunk sooner, heavy and dull and nearly
unconscious. He would slump down in his chair
and for a long time the older man would not try

to rouse him. The older man would sit and finish
his drink, curiously more alive than before, the
skin of his face rich, intensely calm. "Ol' Swans,"
he might say at last, reaching out to pat the boy's
shoulder. As the boy shook his head in an effort
to break the stupor the sergeant smiled, gently.
"Little drunk, aren't yuh? Well, so'm I. It's all
right, you're a good man, yes you are, a good man,
the best." He would try to ruffle the boy's hair
and Swanson would sway backward in the chair.

"Yuh tired, huh? Poor devil, all drunk and tired.
We're gonna go, the old sergeant an Tom is gonna
leave this joint. C'mon Tom, let me hoist you up.
C'mon and get your arm up here where I can get
hold of yuh."

"Leave me a minute," mumbled the boy.
"Don't, I can make it."

"You can't make it without the sarge. You're
drunk, boy."

"I'm all right." And as he stumbled toward the
door, the older man caught up and forced his head
beneath a shoulder.

"Just hold on to the old sarge and we'll make it
fine. No, no, just hold on an let me get you to the
car."

Outside, the boy would wrench loose and stumble into the back seat of the Hudson.

Sometimes when they were drunk and leaving a
café there was a heavy, watching quiet from the
scattered French patrons. In the midst of supporting
the boy the sergeant might suddenly let him
loose, and while Swanson lurched toward the door

the sergeant would stand and look disdainfully
around him. "What're yuh lookin at?" he would
spit at their foreign blankness, standing like he
wanted to fight, feet apart, no longer swaying, his
face bright red from drink. "What yuh think
you're lookin at?"

And he appeared powerful even in his drunkenness, the barrel chest moving slow beneath his
shirt as he looked narrowly over the room.

"I just can't go tonight, sergeant. I'm beat, I
swear, I just can't make it."

"What, you tired?" He turned abruptly toward
the boy's desk, where the afternoon light spread
over Swanson's haggard face. "You tired or sore
or what is it?"

The boy held his hand to his forehead and answered almost inaudibly. "I'm dead tired is all."

"Yeah? Well stay in if that's what you want. Get
some sleep if you're tired." He stalked about the
office with his cap in his hand. "Jesus, I'm not
tired. Hell, I got twenty years on you and I feel
fine."

"I can't help it."

"You're sore about something. Is that it?"

"Christ," murmured the boy. "Look, please—."

"Please! Please what! If you're sore about something, tell me."

"I'm not going out tonight. I'm going to bed,"
said the boy flatly.

"All right, fine. Just don't be sayin one thing
and thinkin another." He moved restlessly about

the room. Because it was this time of day, late
afternoon, he was most real. He was tentative, easily hurt, and his face now was full of hurt as he
wandered about the office, and Swanson could not
help feeling half a traitor. He got up and as he
went toward the door the sergeant grabbed his
arm. "Look, I can see you're tired, all right. I
guess I haven't got any sense at all, thinking I'm a
young dynamo or something. Sure, get some
sleep." The boy nodded in agreement but the sergeant held his arm a moment longer. He chuckled.
"You're not sore, are you?"

"Christ, what have I got to be sore about?" He
hated to see the sergeant like this. He nearly had
to wrench his arm free before he could open the
door and leave the office.

But it was very rarely that the sergeant lost his
toughness. These soft moments of pleading were
quick and fragile, passing invariably into a heavy,
bullish resentment. And that too would pass. His
actions were mostly those of a man on top, over-
riding. Even talking about his sickness, his heart,
even then it was in a strong way, almost an accusation against the world. He spoke of it when the
boy seemed to be drawing away from him, and
those times were coming more and more often.
Sitting together in some bar, the boy would fall
into silences that became longer and heavier with
each passing night. The sergeant's talk did not
seem to touch him, as if he had sunk back into a
brooding world of his own. He would sip at his
drink with a vacantness that infuriated the other

man. "Jesus Christ, snap out of it, will yuh? What
the hell you dreamin about?"

"Nothing."

"Yuh sure as hell are doing something. You
look like you're fifty miles away. What is it? Yuh
thinkin about that Frenchy, what's her name, that
Solange?"

Perhaps it was Solange he was thinking of, not
solidly, but in a fleeting vague way, Solange and
the distant impossible world into which she had
drifted. The sound of her name would cause a
quick, clear pain, enough so that he could lay
down his drink and come back to the moment.

"I don't know what I was thinking about, but I
know one thing, I've had enough cognac for the
night. I'm ready to go."

"Go. Go! My God, we just got here."

"All right. It's your car so I've got to wait, but
I don't want anything more to drink."

"Sure, do what you want. That's your business,"
the sergeant said, drinking up his own cognac and
waving for another.

"Look," he said after another drink, "I don't
know what's eating you but I know one thing and
that's this. If something gets on your mind and
you start feeling sorry for yourself, then you ain't
worth the powder to blow you to hell. I never
thought you were that kind of guy, the kind that
would get sorry for yourself, and it looks like
that's what's happened. I don't have no idea what
your trouble is and I don't know if I would even
want to hear. Shit. Don't you think that every-

body's got their own problems? Shit. Right now, right this minute I got more honest pain than you or anybody knows about." He tapped his shirt front. "Swanson, I got a ticker that could go out this minute. Sometimes I can hear it like the beating of a drum, sometimes there ain't nothin but silence and I just sit there waiting for it to beat again, and boy, I can wake up in the morning with the whole thing tight as a ball. You didn't know that," he accused, passing over the fact that he had spoken of it several times before. "You didn't know it because I got more sense than to bitch and complain and feel sorry for myself."

And because lately Swanson had begun to hear it often, what sympathy he felt was stilted, almost cruel. "You ought to see the medics."

"The medics baloney. Listen, you think I'm shittin you, don't you?"

"No," he said, unable to follow the cruel instinct further.

The sergeant eyed him with an expression close to hate. "Think what you want," he said softly. He turned away and held his shirt front again, his face profiled and mute, and as he held his own shirt he seemed to be waiting, straining, and then suddenly a flash of pain crossed his face, his flesh jumping with a quickness that could only be real. He stared into Swanson's alarm, speaking in a tight whisper of pain, shaking his head with the cruelty of proof. "Any time, boy, it can happen any time."

The boy watched as if stunned, and then his cheeks sprang alive with concern, horror, and as he jumped from his chair to go for help the sergeant's hand waved him down, the grimace of pain easing some. "No doctor," he demanded, still choked. "You hear me, no doctor."

After a moment it had passed. His shoulders eased down and he spoke slowly but without effort. "It comes fast and it goes fast. I get excited like that and it comes on."

"Listen, I should get a doctor!"

"Not on your life," he growled, the firmness of it leaving no room for explanation, and as if to show his contempt for the whole incident he picked up his glass and drained it.

"God, how about the drinking? Shouldn't you take it easy?"

"Swanson, you have no more to say about what I do than the man in the moon." He motioned to the proprietress for another cognac.

"Look, I'm sorry if anything I've done has upset you. It hasn't been intentional, I promise you that."

"Yeah, yeah, forget it, Swanson. A little sickness don't bother me. I'll tell you what bothers me," he said contemptuously. "It's guys that think they can pull the wool over my eyes."

"How do you mean?"

"Don't give me that, don't give me that innocent crap. What do you take me for Swanson, some kind of patsy?"

"Listen, I swear to almighty God I don't know what you're talking about."

"Yeah, yeah, forget it, Swanson. Maybe I've had you figured wrong right from the start." Disgusted, he turned away from the boy, but he turned quickly back. "Look, I don't give a flying frig what you do. But it was getting so that I had a little confidence in you, and then you give me this pile of horseshit."

If it was ludicrous, still Swanson could only feel genuinely upset. All his resolve and momentary certainties, all the clean determination to get up and leave the place—all that was softened and dirtied in his own confusion. "Good Lord, I'm telling the truth, really, Sergeant, I wasn't trying to do anything to rub you wrong."

"All right, all right," answered Callan with a wheeze of condescension. "Just drink down your drink and try to relax." He sat watching the boy's let-down uncertainty, and his voice was resigned yet demanding. "C'mon there boy, drink up and snap out of it."

And once again he would be drawn painfully back, back into a thickness that swirled faster with each drink or mated word. So many times, in so many ways, his resolve was crushed. Always he would be swept back, back into the red magic of the man's strange force. He could feel himself being drawn, slipping, going. And as he felt it there would be another moment of struggle, a last moment of struggle. He had to get away, he had to tear away. It was like a cry, a prayer, and yet it too was softened by confusion. Even if he went off by himself, would it do any good, would it stop the hurt!

And the confusion made it worse, it would seem to hurtle him forward, crazily, until once again he was staggering and flushed, and he would curse the room and its people, as if to make himself right, and through it all he could hear the other man's voice, urging him on. "Tell 'em boy, tell 'em." He would drink again, he could feel again the intensity of himself, he could feel it growing, bursting. And as it went on, as everything was once again clenched and tight and colored—it was then that the hurt would suddenly twist anew. It would come as from the outside. It would plunge him down into his chair, flooded with loss, with shame, and he could feel his face against the table and he could hear the terrible beginning of his own prayers, muffled, pleading, incoherent.

Chapter Nineteen

As so many times in the past, he stood on the stone bridge and watched the wide swirling brownness of the Garonne. He remembered that he used to think of it as his river, his city. And now it seemed fearfully strange. He looked beyond the expanse of river into the gray and spreading city, and like a traveler returning to his birthplace he wondered at the passage of time and the unfolding of events that separated him now from the richness and moment of the thousand slow memories which it had all once held.

Even the road into town—that too had been cold and separate, empty of the old adventure and joy. An outsider to the dearness of his own world. He felt that. He felt the week-end pass in his wallet was a lie. He felt a thief in taking it without telling Callan. He felt, for a moment, that he must go down off the bridge and back to the camp.

But with an ironic discipline he turned and walked into the city. It was late November now, and still the real rains had not come. The concrete

of the streets and sidewalks and buildings was dry
and shiny beneath the afternoon sun, and as he
walked through the crowds he had the impression
that this should not be, that the weather had
carried too long until now it was pending and
unreal, and the unreality seemed to spread into the
people themselves, the way they went on as always
before, hurrying, shouting, honking their horns
beneath the false bright sky.

He would go first to Café Jacque and have a
drink, and then he would call Solange. He had
planned it like that in a hundred moments of
quick yearning and remorse, the café with its old
familiarity, the beautiful clink of the jitney as it
dropped down through the telephone box, the
excited waiting, and then the warm and living
voice. And yet, as he approached Café Jacque, his
plan seemed vacant, impotent, as false as the
weather.

For a Saturday afternoon, the little bar was
crowded. A woman and several men were perched
upon the stools, and two of the three tables were
filled. He made his way up to the bar and caught
the eye of Madame Jacque, who took her hands
from a sink of rinse water and shook them dry in
a kind of greeting.

"Ah, comment-tu-va?" she said, smiling, turning
quickly to fill a glass for another customer. He
could see, in that instant, that she had forgotten
his name. It made his heart catch and drop. "Tom,
Tom Swanson," he muttered darkly. "Monsieur
Tom."

She came back to him, smiling still, and he ordered his cognac and when she set it in front of
him he took it to the one empty table. He didn't
want to remain standing where she would feel
obliged to make conversation, false inquiries, some
safe and stilted questions, all the while trying to
place him. Well, what had he expected? How long
had it been now? Six weeks? More than that, even.
Was she supposed to be a lifelong friend?

He drank down the cognac and watched the little cubicle where the telephone was. And how
would that go? Probably the same, he thought
dully.

He had another cognac before he made the call,
and as he dialed and listened to the spaced buzz-
ing there was not the excitement that he had expected and the dullness continued like a forced
thing.

It was not Solange who answered, but her
mother, and when he asked for Solange in French
the mother answered that she was out. When
would she be in? It was not known exactly but
could one take a message. No. Your name, Monsieur? He told his name and said good-by and
thank you and hung up the phone.

It was when he hung up the phone that the
dullness left him. Disappointment flooded over
him so quick and complete that he clutched at the
receiver as for support. He felt as if his heart
were hung in a quivering shell. A wine-breathed
Frenchman peered into the cubicle and pointed
toward the phone, and it took a sick, leaping ef-

fort to shoulder past him into the wide strange-
ness of the bar.

Then he was in the streets among the lying motion of people and vehicles, among the lying
sounds of horns and motors and voices, passing
through the ghost world from bar to bar.

How long had it been since he was drunk by
himself? A long, long time, and now he could get
drunk by himself and by God he was drunk already and the hell with the world's million lies.
She wasn't there, that girl, and he hadn't expected
her to be and why should she be there and what
difference anyhow? Hadn't he come into Bordeaux
just to know that with the girl it was finished?
Hadn't he needed and yearned downward toward
that final knowing? Sure, yes, why else would he
come? He could know things now even more for
sure, and if it hurt, Jesus let it hurt, at least he
saw. Couldn't he see there in the lying face of
each passing Frenchman Jesus look at them Jesus
another cognac so he didn't have to see down the
bar, see them laughing and backslapping, each
drink that stood in front of them a lie each hearty
laugh a lie Christ dear Christ another cognac to
blind the sight of waiters winking at women each
wink and gesture a lie, worse, to shut out the
rough voices rough features the lie the lie oh
Christ dear God almighty it was everywhere.

He saw Captain Loring. He saw him through
the window of a nearly deserted café, and his heart
leaped with the pervading cruelty of his new and
bitter knowledge. He stumbled into the café, a

cold dark place, empty save for the captain who sat alone at a round marble-topped table near the center of the room. He guided himself toward the man, his hand brushing along the cold surface of the deserted bar. A glass and a bottle of cognac were set nakedly on the captain's table, and the man's hands were palms down beside them. He was sitting upright, and his head, like a dead man's, hung loosely forward. The boy eased away from the bar out toward the island of the captain's table and he grabbed for the back of a chair and braced himself and stared at the drooping Indian face. He set himself down, quietly, carefully, and a ripple passed down the skin of the man's cheek, like a sign of awareness to a presence, like the spasm of a horse's hide at the touch of a fly. Swanson sat there, squinting, leaning into the thickness and pulse of the man's isolation.

The captain's head raised up slowly, a labor, and his dull eyes opened to take in the boy. "Yes," he whispered, a long sound tainted with wonder, a wheeze emerging from deep in his throat into a full-molded word. "Yes, it's Swanson."

The boy nodded, his whole upper body moving in dumb affirmation. "Swanson," he mumbled. Then neither of them spoke. But there was sound and rhythm in the silence between them. The captain's palm rolled over on the table, an offer to share the cognac.

The boy ignored it, staring past the averted gaze into the thin, brown face. "You're a goddamn coward," he said.

No emotion showed from the other man.
Crudely, with effort, he poured out a drink.

"You stay away because you're scared of him,"
breathed the boy.

And once again the Indian head labored up to
meet the boy's pulsing stare. Something occurred
in the area of the eyes, a passing over, a shadow
as imperceptible as the moment of its occurrence,
and his mouth opened then closed and the difference in their ages and rank disappeared as he
finally formed a smile, almost kind, and spoke
with slow, paced care. "Yes, I stay away because
I'm afraid. And you, what is it with you?"

He could not remember in the morning where
or how they found him. Perhaps he had wandered
and staggered back toward the Bar Jacque. All he
could remember was her frightened face and their
voices from the near distance.

"I tell you, Paul, he's more than drunk."

"It's nothing, he's only drunk, Solange, mon
Dieu!"

"I know him! I know him!" and her voice was
tearful and pleading. "He's ill, I know it."

There was arguing and then he could feel their
hands on him, hers soft and tentative, his with
persuasive force, and once he hurled him away
and stared madly into the girl's white face; then
once again they were holding him and he could
feel the core of violence in his shouts and the violence in his elbows as they lashed against the sober, infuriating grip of the man, Paul. They were

pulling him up a stairway and then he was in a room alone with Solange and for a moment he was quieter and she was easing his shoulders onto a bed and whispering to him, "Don't say that, I'm not going to let you down, Tom, I promise you I won't."

Her lips were brushing his cheek and the violence roared again and he had hold of her tightly, wrestling her down onto the bed with a warped cry in his throat, his hands clutching with violent purpose at her body, the foulness of his own breath coming back to him from the crook of her straining neck. "Please! Please!" came her voice, "don't do this, please, try to lie back and sleep," and then she was struggling against him, coolly, precisely, and then she was free and speaking again. "No, no, I'm not running away, but it's all wrong, you don't want me now, just lie back and sleep, do you hear me, do you understand, oh darling Tom, Tom I love you, please understand. I'll be here in the morning, I'll come in the morning."

Her footsteps moved away and the light in the room was snapped off, and it seemed a long time before the door opened and closed.

He remembered these things in the morning, in the first moments of waking. His eyes opened onto the strange ceiling and it came back to him in a black rush and he turned into his pillow and prayed for a fresh awakening that would make a dream of what he had remembered. But the heaviness was in his system, irrevocably, and as he forced himself up from the bed he moaned as with the weight of it.

Except for his shoes he was fully dressed. His shoes were placed neatly beside a chair and he put them on and went into the bathroom that opened off the room, running the water for a minute before he splashed it on his face. When he'd finished he went back to the bed and sat down. Across, there was a large balcony-like window and two rays of sun stabbed in and fanned over the carpeted floor. She must have brought him to her home. He thought again of the night before. It couldn't have been true, what she had said there at the end. It was out of kindness, a way of quieting him down. Of course it was out of kindness, she had sense, she could see inside him, there was nothing there she would want. He didn't belong in a house like this, he didn't belong in the same house with a good girl and a good family. He wanted only to go out the door and down the stairs and away.

There was a knock on the door and her voice. "I heard you moving around. May I come in?"

For a moment longer he sat on the bed. He got up and opened the door and she was standing there with a smile.

"Good morning," he said heavily.

"My room is right under yours and I could hear you getting up."

He stood aside without looking at her. "Come on in."

She came into the room and sat in the chair by the little reading table. "I hope you're not angry with me for bringing you here. Paul said you were just drunk but I thought that you were ill so I brought you."

"I was just drunk, I guess. I hope bringing me doesn't make any trouble for you with your parents."

"Oh, no, they understand." Her hands folded and unfolded in her lap. "They're awfully nice people," she said, smiling, and then she turned nervously and glanced about the room as if it were new to her.

He saw her nervousness and for an instant it drew him toward her. "I hope that I didn't insult you last night."

She turned quickly back to him. "No, of course you didn't."

"I'm sorry, anyway," he said.

"No," she said flatly. She stood up, still glancing about the room. "I came up to show you how to work the hot water in the bathtub. There's a little trick to it."

"Oh . . . well . . . I thought I'd just go right on. I've been enough trouble as it is."

"Oh please, stay and take breakfast with us. I've already told my parents and they're expecting you, and oh, it's no trouble at all, Paul is here with his wife, you know, Valerie, my sister. We're all expecting you."

"I'd better go," he said hurriedly. "Look at my clothes, look how I look," he said, running a hand over his rough cheek, wanting desperately to get out of the room and away from her kindness.

But she stood in front of him and did not move or make any sign. And then he saw her face was pink with hurt. Was it that she was serious? Did she really want him to stay?

"It's been such a long time since I've seen you," she implored. "I thought that maybe you would spend a little time today."

It seemed incredible that after the past night, after a month or more of nothing, she could be standing there asking for his company. He couldn't bring himself to believe that it wasn't sympathy or some part of the goodness of her nature. Yet in her steady gaze there was no trace of benevolence or sympathy and it seemed incredible to him, false even, for there was nothing in himself that she should want.

"Do you really want me to stay?"

"Yes," she urged, and she was becoming brighter, less nervous.

"Well . . . sure . . . your parents, they won't mind?"

"No, not at all!" She stood back. "I already told them we had a guest." She began to laugh. "They're shocked, but nevertheless they insist that you come down for breakfast, and Paul and my sister are here too. They come up from the country to spend week ends with us. Sunday is my father's chance to be at home and he likes the family and people near. And my father speaks English so don't be nervous. Only you can't be angry when he makes jokes at you. He makes jokes at everybody."

"Solange," he said suddenly, "where did you find me last night?"

"Near the Café Jacque," she said. "When I got home and Mother said you had called I made Paul come with me and we went to look for you there."

Inside himself he could feel a strange, reluctant warmth.

"I guess I was plenty drunk."

"Listen, Tom," she said suddenly. She stepped up to him with a hand along his waist. "I know that something's been bothering you. One can't help seeing it. But for this morning, for this one day, won't you try your best to forget it? Won't you try to have this morning all by itself?"

"Sure," he said quickly, and he spoke quickly to cover the shock that her words and tone gave him. "Sure, of course." It shocked him to see her standing there, watching him with even eyes.

"Could you— Could you get me a razor? I'm ashamed, looking like this."

"Don't be ashamed of anything," she said seriously. She paused. And then she became bright again. "I'll get you a razor right away."

When he had taken his bath he went down a flight of stairs and knocked at her door and together they went down to the ground floor. She put a hand through his arm and led him into a large dining room, and from beyond, what was presumably the kitchen, he could hear a flood

of talk and laughter. A swinging door pushed
open and a large man labored through backward,
balancing a tray of dishes, and with him from the
kitchen came the warm smell of coffee and pas-
tries. He placed the tray on the table, looking up
to greet them with an exclamation. "Ah-ha! The
drunkard and his keeper!"

Tom tried to smile. He offered his hand awkwardly across the table.

"Ah, I cannot greet you properly," said the big
man, thrusting out his dough-covered hands for
them to see. "I am covered with bread."

A small, white-haired woman, her face still
young, followed behind him from the kitchen. "It
is Sunday," she explained, "and on Sunday he in-
sists upon being a baker. I am Madame Gerard."
She took his still extended hand. "And this large
man is my husband. Your name is Tom Swanson,
I know, since my daughter is standing there like a
child idiot and not presenting you."

"How do you do?" he said.

Paul, the third voice in the kitchen, came into
the dining room carrying a plate of croissants.
"You see," he explained in French, "he walks, he
talks, he is not dead!"

"Speak English," said Madame Gerard. "You
were five years with it in school. Doesn't Valerie
try to bring you some culture?"

"I refuse to speak English," and he popped one
of the croissants into his mouth. "I will only make
myself a fool and I cannot afford that and Valerie
knows it too."

"But you understand French," asked Madame Gerard, turning to Tom.

"Certainly he does," said Paul. "He is like Solange, very, very intelligent. Only he is a primitive, I suspect, what do you call them? A man who does not realize his intelligence?"

"I speak excellent English," called the father, who had returned to the kitchen and was banging among the pots and pans. "In nineteen-twenty-seven I was six months in St. Louis, Missouri." In a loud, surprisingly true voice he launched into a rendition of the "St. Louis Blues."

"He will never forget that six months in St. Louis," said Madame Gerard. She spoke directly to Tom. "They make him into a grand adventurer. But sit down, both of you." She gestured at him depreciatingly, at the way he stood awkwardly behind the chair. "You make me nervous standing like that." She bustled away and Valerie came out from the kitchen and the four young people sat down. Valerie was perhaps a year or two older than Solange, a blond girl with the same open good looks as her sister. She smiled a greeting.

"Now tell me," said Paul, "how can you be so cheerful so soon after all that whisky? I can't understand you Americans. You drink whisky like some insanity. It should be savored, gently, like a woman." He formed his mouth into a cup and his fingers filtered down imaginary drops.

Swanson didn't have to answer, for Madame Gerard appeared with oranges and more croissants and the doctor with a glass pitcher of coffee and a moment later with a pitcher of steaming milk. The table was scattered with a variety of light foods. "I wish you could have my bread!" boomed the doctor. "But it is a labor that takes time. All day! Will you be here for dinner?" and without leaving time for an answer he exclaimed enthusiastically, "If you are here for dinner you will taste my bread!"

Madame Gerard took a chair by Paul and eventually the clatter of pots in the kitchen diminished and the doctor re-entered to sit at the head of the table. "In the week days we employ a maid but that is not so amusing. Now we must eat. Any time, any second," he said, threatening them all with a spoon, "I may be called away on a matter of great urgency. A finger without a fingernail! A nose that bleeds! Ah, life is severe!" With that he took a long draught of coffee and began with utmost precision to slice away the skin of an orange.

"Tell us now," said the mother. "You are a soldier at the American camp?"

He nodded and put down his spoon. "Yes, I was drafted about a year and a half ago."

"And in America, from what state do you come?"

"From California," he said.

"That's a beautiful state," boomed the father. "I have not been there, of course, but I have read, I hear, I imagine!"

"In truth," said the mother again, "we know all

this already, for this girl so silent now on occasion talks a great deal." Solange had been very quiet beside him, he realized it then, quiet and bright-faced. She seemed almost proud.

"But it is good to hear it from you," continued Madame Gerard. "Solange is one of the purest people I know, and when those kind are enthusiastic, facts do not have much to do with the telling of a story."

There was no irony or sarcasm in the description of her daughter. The mother looked upon her fondly as she spoke, yet with a certain withdrawn respect, as if she were as much a guest as a member of the family. He could see that, and he could feel Solange beside him, and suddenly he knew that inside himself it was better.

"And you," said Madame Gerard, "do you have a large family?"

"Yes, there's five of us."

They were all waiting as though they expected him to continue, and suddenly the bad feeling from the night before, the restraint, the caution, left him. He wanted very much to be talking to these people. Even Paul was waiting with a perched-forward interest.

"In a way it's strange. You people make it easy to think of them. So many things are the same. You know, there's a swinging door between our kitchen and dining room and it's exactly like that one. I've seen my father push through it the same way you did, sir, backward and carrying a stack of dishes. Then the way we go about having Sunday breakfast at home, that's nearly the same too. We all fix what we want for ourselves, eggs, pancakes, whatever we feel like. And before my sister was married that would make five of us in the kitchen. There'd be a lot of confusion in that kitchen, bumping into one another, raising cain over who could use the griddle or who had the butter, but we were happy when we were doing it. Kind of happy abusing each other. And then we sat around the table afterwards with a pot of coffee. Well, it was like—" He paused, trying to search out the answer for himself. "It was like we were all strangers for a moment. It was like we weren't a family but separate people around a table. We would be having our coffee, looking at each other, taking nothing for granted, and for a moment we would be the most beautiful kind of strangers."

He had forgotten himself as he talked, and he leaned back slightly in his chair and the others watched him. "Do you know what I mean?" He said it almost to himself.

They had all watched him closely, Madame Gerard with a curious smile. "Certainly we do," she said. "And we approve!"

"I approve!" seconded the father. His hand, holding a roll, had been suspended halfway to his mouth, and he shoved in the roll with an air of finality. The boy, becoming aware of the silence that had surrounded the description of his family, laughed again, self-consciously.

"You see, he is a primitive," said Paul, who could not have followed the talk but had watched the faces of the others.

After the breakfast the two of them walked to the back of the house where there was a long garden colored with the high red of roses and webbed with gravel paths. He sat down on a bench and she sat beside him. For a few minutes they were quiet, and yet it was alive, he could feel the closeness of her. A soft excitement was going through him. He looked up at the sky and the sky held an early-day blue which set off the green and red of the garden. No colors can clash in nature, he thought. He lowered his head and smiled. It was good to have a thought like that, so distinct and separate from any inside pull. It had been a long time. And it had been a long time since he had felt this gentle, free excitement. Yet he was almost afraid to let it go further, to let it bubble and open and . . . and this girl next to him.

"Solange . . ." He tried to turn toward her but he could only look ahead, down one of the gravel paths. "Being in this home . . . being with you . . . it makes me feel better than in a long time."

She sat quiet without answering.

"Solange. Last night I know I acted badly. I was feeling a lot of different things and I know how badly I acted." In the silence he looked steadily down the garden path. Already he was confused and yet he wanted almost desperately to go on with it. "But last night you said—I— Did you say that—" He couldn't look at her and he couldn't finish it.

"I do love you," she said softly.

He turned quickly. She was looking at the garden, her face still, delicate. In his chest he felt a release, a great beginning whiteness. "Solange . . . I—" He took hold of her hand.

"I do," she said again.

"Oh Solange. God!" He took hold of her, hold of her close. "Oh God, God, so much has happened out there, I want to tell you, oh God, listen to me you good girl, listen to me and I don't know how to say anything, it's that camp, it got to me, there's this thing happening, it's had me blind, I couldn't think, it made everything wrong—"

"Don't. Don't tell me now."

"I've got to tell you and I don't know if I can. It's all so damned confused, but I see it, in my heart I see it, I swear. Oh God, Solange, I've been in so damn close, so damn close I couldn't think." He wrenched himself back on the bench, trying to catch himself and slow his excitement. All about him the sky was blue. "There's this sergeant. I see what's happening, God, I think I've seen all along. But I couldn't say it, I couldn't say it to myself, God I was in so close. It's been covering everything, it's made everything dark. Last night was the worst, I was like a madman. It's this thing with this sergeant, I knew what was happening but I couldn't say it." He took her hand, hard. "I couldn't say it," he repeated. "I was beginning to doubt myself."

She could see the release in him, without fully understanding it, and her hand pressed into his.

"But it's all right!" He was excited, bursting. "It's going to be all right, I see it now, I know it, I know it. Oh God, you good girl. You and one morning, oh God, how I've needed it. It's been . . . like being pulled under, oh God, that's what it's like. Just a day, a pause, a breath, oh God, how I've needed it." He was breathing heavily, as if his chest were being ripped open and evacuated. Her hand was upon his cheek and then around to the back of his neck and she was kissing his cheeks and lips and he was kissing her hard with the same flow of whiteness that was bursting inside him.

"Oh," she whispered, "stay here all day, stay tonight again."

He kissed her again and then he put his hands on her shoulder and held her and as he held her he looked past out into the garden without seeing. "No, it's better that I go back now on the noon train."

"But Tom," she whispered.

"No, listen, it's the right thing, I know. It's the thing I've got to do."

"But won't you stay?"

He looked at her and he was happy. There was a new calmness. "Listen. Solange. It's so good. . . . It's so good. I've got to get clean. I'm not ready yet."

"Not ready?" She repeated it and he could hear how foolish the words sounded, and yet it was so important, a part of what he was saying, and she had to understand.

And she looked at him and her face showed that she could see and she nodded and pressed in slow and close. "But I'm going to be ready," he whispered, "I swear to you."

Chapter Twenty

The rains came in the night and they continued through the night, bringing a thick whiteness to the morning. It was not an erratic rain, for it came in large satisfied drops that splashed single on the earth and sank deep so that the wetness was fixed and confident. It came warm and steady.

The sergeant came into the office and unbuttoned his slicker with stiff, slow fingers and he spoke before he had gotten it off. "You think you put something over on me!" He spoke with his mouth half-closed, a growl.

At first the boy did not look at him. "You don't usually talk in the mornings," he said.

"Shut up!" roared the older man, staring at the seated boy, quivering in the wake of his own voice. He tore off the slicker and threw it on a chair and turned back. "So," he whispered. "So . . . I can court-martial you for taking a pass without telling me."

"I don't think you can. I followed the posted

214

regulations. I was off duty, I took my pass out of the box, I signed the sign-out ledger and checked out with the gate guard."

The older man's lips were trembling. "Don't talk to me," he whispered. His lips trembled slightly and his face, still damp from rain, was a glistening gray color. "You went into Bordeaux. You went outa here like a sneaky rat. You went to see that little bitch."

The boy's expression was grim, ready. Callan stared down and his mouth moved dryly and his temples were stretched. "You did that, didn't you?"

"Yes."

The sergeant stood planted in front of the desk and his hands crept out and hooked the edge like red and white claws and his head inched forward until it loomed with all its wet grayness, the surface of the skin alive, breathing. Then he was motionless. There was no motion in the room. He stared at the boy. Slowly, carefully, his hands pulled away from the desk and he stepped back.

All day long he watched. He watched from the other desk as he had not done since the boy's first weeks in the office. Swanson felt the eyes. They were a heat across his forehead, his heart, his navel. They ached along his neck and spine. Nothing touched between them, no comings or goings, neither the business of soldiers nor the presence of the captain. The rain was steady all day but in the room there was no sound, not until late afternoon.

"You're not going with me for a beer?"

"No."

"Because you're tired?"

"No."

There was a thick moment in which there could have been more talk. And it passed.

The boy ate his dinner in the mess hall, and with his head bowed he stayed outside the hum of the table. He ate and went to his hut. In the hut he cleaned out his locker and re-hung his uniforms. He took a cloth and polish and sat on his bed and polished his parade boots. The tar-papered roof received the raindrops with a hollow *ping*. There was no wind with the rain and the stove sucked and bloated and the room was prickly warm. There was a knock on the door.

The men in the hut looked up, startled, and then they turned to Tom. He looked at each of them, clearly. "It's Sergeant Callan," he said.

He put down his boots and walked across the room and opened the door. The sergeant stood outside in the heavy rain. "Come out here. I want to talk to you."

Swanson stepped down onto the wet wooden sidewalk.

"What do you think you're doing?" breathed the sergeant.

"I'm doing what I want," said the boy.

As in the office, Callan's lips were trembling. "Don't give me any shit," he warned.

The boy felt the rain running down his face and neck.

"I'm telling you, Swanson, I'm gonna do it to yuh good."

"That's all right." The boy was trembling too.

"I'm telling you, Swanson, I'll fix you so that you'll never forget it."

Through the thick, heavy rain they stared at each other.

"You'll never have another pass from this company. You know that right now, don't you?"

"Sergeant." His voice was choked. "I'm ready. . . . I'm standing. . . . I've got hate. . . . Sergeant, you do what you want."

Water rolled off the sergeant's thick face, separate drops going slow down his forehead and cheeks.

"Boy," he said. "Boy . . ." In the hardness of his voice there was a terrible catch, and there was a beginning, a suggestion of collapse on his face, a moment without breath when it could all fall with a shattered wail. But he lowered his head. His shoulders squared. "Why do you do this?"

"I don't want to talk."

"Why do you do this?" he said, his voice flat and eerie. "You shouldn't want to be like that," he said, and there was a pale flicker of smile at the corners of his mouth. "No, you shouldn't," he said softly and then the smile became full and strange and his eyes were fixed wide. He turned and walked off through the rain.

Swanson went back into the hut and the others waited. "It was Callan," he said. The tremble was still in his hands. He could look at each of them, at Pop and Sam and Aldous, and he could see them wanting to know. "It's nothing. I can't talk. It's okay, it's all right."

They watched him quietly. When he went to his bunk they turned away.

When he was alone in the Orderly room the next morning he saw the pass box sitting on Callan's desk. It had been taken down from on top of the file cabinet. He went over and looked into it. His pass was still there. Then the door slammed and the sergeant was standing behind him.

"Yeah, I haven't taken your little pass."

He shrugged off his raincoat without glancing at Swanson. For once, his uniform was not immaculate. The knot of his tie was hurried and out of place and the lapel of his coat was soiled. "No," he said, "I'm gonna let you keep that little pass. Poor Swanson. Poor Swanson without his pass." He came over to the desk and slammed shut the box. "You know why I'm gonna let you keep it? Because you're a miserable little snot. Because you're the kind of cry-baby punk that would go squealing to the IG. I can hear it, oh Christ, I can hear it now! That bad man has taken my pass, oh please help me Mr. IG because I'm so young and pure and he's so bad." The sergeant leaned toward him. "That's what you'd do, ain't it, Private? You cry-baby punks are all the same. Let me say this . . . take your little holidays to Bordeaux, take all you want. But don't do nothing that I can get you for. Because boy—I'll get you." He looked hard at Swanson's quiet, tight-lipped face and then he turned away as a man turns away after spitting. He looked quickly through the mail and left the office.

Callan came in and out through the day, staying only long enough to do the necessary work. He ignored the boy. He would be in the office ten or fifteen minutes and then for several hours he would be gone. He did not even glance toward Swanson, that day or in those to follow. The boy did his work with a quietness that was careful, fragile.

Men were beginning to come loud into the office, loitering by the stove in the sergeant's absence.

"He's leavin home base quite a bit, ain't he? I guess you don't mind, heh Swanson? Or do you?" Then, turning away quickly: "Jesus, lookit that rain. Why does a man wanta be outside in a rain like that?"

Once or twice the sergeant returned to find several men standing around the stove and he roared into their quick, guilty silence, "These are duty hours, ain't they? You men all aimin to go to jail?"

Ashamed, like frightened children, they shuffled back to the mess hall, the supply room, back to their duty posts.

But Callan never spoke to Swanson, even to warn him against allowing slackers in the office. He would perform some quick task and leave without a word.

The men would come again.

"You know what he's been doing?" one of them would say. "He's been going around and watching men workin. Christ, it's enough to drive a man nuts. Jess said that he's been comin out to the depot and he just stands there in the rain watchin 'em and then he might catch 'em at somethin or see somethin he don't think is right, and by God, Jess said he comes on like a lion, gives 'em hell up and down until they is so goddamned nervous they're afraid to make a move. And I know, Jesus! I was sortin some stuff in the supply room and I musta been at it ten minutes or so when I look around and there he's been standin the whole time. Christ!"

They came in and told Swanson these things and they looked at him curiously, as if he could add more.

"It must be kinda tough, spendin all day in the same office with him. But you're pretty chummy, ain't you? How about that, Swanson? You do some drinkin with him, don't yuh?"

Swanson could look around and see the hidden accusation with its line of cruelty. But somehow that part of it no longer bothered him; he was slow with it. Yet there was something else about it. It was strange that none of them knew the man. He could look around and feel them waiting. But his quiet was careful, fragile.

"My guess," said one of them, "is that he's been drinking. I mean drinking on duty. He's got that look in his eyes, but God almighty, you'd expect a man to loosen up with a little booze in his belly. And no one can say that he's done any loosening up. You know, Swanson, it seems—"

But somebody warned that Callan's jeep had driven into the parking lot, and the loiterers moved quick out of the office.

The boy spent the evenings in the hut, and he wrote letters and he polished his boots. He stroked his boots with a dry cloth, spitting on the toe, then moving the cloth slow and circular. The shine was like glass and it was increasing.

"I think I'll shine mine too," said Aldous Brown, standing up. With a pleased and secret hand he pulled his boots from beneath his bunk and began to clean the dust from them. None of them spoke much to Tom now. It was as if they sensed a new tone to his quiet and they were as careful in their manner as he. All of them. Even Sam. Even Sam lay quiet and waiting.

"You went to the city las' week end, didn't you?" said Aldous.

"Yes, I did."

"You enjoyed it, didn't yuh?"

He paused with the motion of the dry cloth. "Sure."

"Well, thas just fine," continued the slow Negro voice.

The stove warmed the corners of the room. The men and the air seemed very still.

"I been seein that sergeant out at the depot. He been comin out there. I was thinkin," he said.

"I was thinkin how he looked mean . . . different mean."

With his head lowered over the work, the boy nodded.

"Yes," said the Negro softly. "He certainly do."

Three days, then four passed, and the boy took his pass and went to see Solange in Bordeaux. After that he went more often, every night or two. They sat together in a little den at the rear of the house and the boy made a fire in the fireplace and they talked. He sat next to her on a sofa, and the fire had the gentleness of a warm hand.

"You seem happier every time," she said, but then she stopped, as if it were wrong to speak of it.

There were times when he was riding into Bordeaux that impulse made him turn and look back down the road, and sometimes he thought he saw the distant flash of the American car, the Hudson. He would not let himself scan the road, but he would turn back and sit rigid while the city drew closer. When he got off he would not look back but he would make a web through the city streets, walking rapidly. And in the mornings there was a sign, quick, fearful—a sign on the sergeant's face as he walked in and then out of the office.

Chapter Twenty-One

In the hut one morning they woke to find Pop Henneken missing from his bunk. As they got up and dressed, all of them were apprehensive, for there had never been a time when the old man had not made it in from his wine drunks in the meadow. Then Ivy the stove-keeper came bursting through the door and they knew. They knew before he had opened his mouth.

"That man's in jail," said Ivy with an excited finger pointed toward the unused bunk. "He went got hisself caught an it was by that man there." The finger swung to the direction of the Orderly room.

Swanson questioned him sharply. "What do you mean he's in jail?"

"He's in jail, thas what. He been at the MPs since twelve las' midnight an that Sergeant Callan, he say that ol' Pop ain't gonna never leave that place until he proper court-martialed. He say old Pop is unfit for 'sociation with soldiers of this comp'ny an that he's gonna be run right outa the service."

"What's he charged with?"

"He charged with drunk," said the excited Negro. "He charged with drunk and bein off camp without no pass and bein outa uniform, but that ain't all, the sergeant, he got lot a things lumped up together an he say he gonna Section Eight ol' Pop right outa the service."

"And Callan was the one that caught him?"

"I tell you yes. It weren't no MP or night guard or nobody but that Callan hisself. He got him somewhere out there in that black meadow las' night!"

Ivy was boiling with his recitation, so excited that he ignored the reactions of the others, staring at the unused bunk as if it were a coffin.

Swanson dressed quickly and when he arrived in the Orderly room the sergeant was already back from the MPs. For once he did not turn away from the boy. He was grinning.

"So you're going to do it," said Swanson tightly.

"Do what?"

The boy was too choked to speak and he brushed past Callan without carrying it on. Even to stand and look at the man made his body ache with challenge.

"Are you talking about Henneken?" asked the sergeant, facing away, his voice pleasant.

Swanson sat down at his desk and fought with the rush of profanity that cracked at his throat, and when the sergeant turned and saw his expression his smile broadened.

"Yes, I suppose you're talking about old Pop, aren't you. What did you ask? If I was going to do it? Well, I don't quite understand what you mean by that, but I do know that certain measures will be taken in the old fellow's case. Most likely he'll be subjected to a Section Eight board. I'm going to run him out of the Army," he added sharply, and as he said that his voice and manner changed. His smile seemed to bear forward like a weapon. "He's through, Swanson, do you understand, through six months before his retirement. Today you can begin to type up the court-martial papers, and Swanson, it's got to be carefully done, no errors are allowed in this type of thing. Something to fill your time, eh boy? A little work for lazy rainy days."

The sergeant began to move stiffly around the room, the smile more grotesque with each fixed and passing second, his fingers like clutching, brittle sticks against his pants leg. "You see, boy, you see how it is."

He paused in the middle of the room and the evenness of his deep breathing was frightening. "And you, Swanson, I been thinking about you. This job of company clerk has been allowing too many liberties. You're going to start doing a few things . . . stand formations and inspections for instance. Understand? Understand Swanson?" He leered at the boy's rigidness.

"And I'm going to put you on a few rosters.

CQ and night guard. How do you like that?" he challenged, pausing when he saw the boy's hate, then hurtling on like a straining athlete. "You don't much like it." He beamed. He made a choked laugh. "Now that's a dirty shame, ain't it? It's a dirty shame that it isn't you who's running this company, huh Swanson?" He pointed his finger, half exaltation, half rage. "But it ain't you, it's me, and by God you're gonna hafta remember that. Aren't you?"

Through the day he was near Swanson's desk with instructions for the preparation of the court-martial papers, and he hovered smiling over the boy's tight silence and when he shoved new papers down onto the desk they were smudged from the wetness of his hands. He was wet and perspiring. When he faced them at evening formation his forehead glistened with the oil of his emotions and he sent them down the company street in a police call, following behind their stooping forms, and all the while his voice roared through their backs. "Get it all, you monkeys, every scrap and butt and wrapper, get it all, yuh hear me, or you'll go back and do it again!"

Pop Henneken was court-martialed less than a week later, and during that period the sergeant generated an aura of excitement that touched even the unwilling. It seemed to emanate from his very person, a leaping, driving force that quickened the movements of his body and gave him the fierceness of a wild and roaming animal. It was as though he was filled with his own effect on others. He roamed down the wooden sidewalks and when he passed men he grinned as he swept through their fat pocket of fear. In the office he would watch the boy's tight-lipped quiet and suddenly the room would fill with his closed and colored laughter.

The court-martial gave Henneken three months of hard labor with a recommendation that his case be further submitted to a Section Eight board. When it was all over there was a change in Callan.

Once again he kept away from the Orderly room and once again he tried to ignore the boy. He still roamed the streets, taking his distant watch of the men at work, but the men could sense that it was a different, listless kind of watching. In the office he tried to ignore the boy, but the eyes would creep upward beneath the dark and silent forehead, and the boy would bend farther into his work and his hands would tighten into the keys of the typewriter. Though sometimes he looked up, and in the man's quick eyes he could see the almost terrifying plea.

Tom did not take the girl out when he went to Bordeaux. They sat in the little den with the fire and in the boy there was a sure and spreading warmth. Yet there was a ring there, a dark ring that bit sharply with each new opening. It would make him draw back. But quietly, closely . . . He could feel the steady warmth.

And there were times . . . when he was walking with her in the evening streets . . . when he
would turn and see a darting shadow . . . times
when he would hold her arm at the glimpse of a
car rounding a corner.

Chapter Twenty-Two

They were talking about the sergeant, almost everybody in the company. They talked about the way
he was drinking, his appearance, the unreasonable-
ness of his orders. At the morning formations, even
then he seemed drunk, his voice gravel-rough, his
stance planted too rigidly. As he outlined the work
for the day his instructions were labored and sometimes incoherent. Only the fiber of meanness remained.

Each time they broke from the stiffness of ranks
they talked anew.

"Sure he's drunk. My God, all you gotta do is
look at him."

"If the IG comes around that man's gonna have
it."

"You know at least before you could always
say he was a soldier."

"Yeah . . . Still, he's no one to screw with."

A current of excitement ran steadily through
the company. Coming back in the trucks for noon
chow the men went first to their buddies who

worked around the company area. They went to
the supply hut or mail room or they talked to Ivy.

"What's he been doing, Ivy? He been around
the company area?"

"How you 'xpect me to know? You think I 'bout
to be following a crazy man?"

"How do you mean, crazy? What's he been doin?"

"Man, don't be askin me nothin." He spoke
impatiently, importantly, excited. "You think I
know anything 'bout a man who go crashin through
the huts tearin up the bunks an sayin he gonna
court-martial the whole goddamn comp'ny 'cause
they can't make no proper bunk?"

They spread through their huts to see the torn-
up bunks, Ivy following close behind. "He calls
that an inspection," said the Negro. "Yes suh,
that's what he called it!"

Each new day brought a tighter air of expectancy. They followed Callan's actions with un-
natural avidness. Among the men there was a
strange coming together, a mean and happy union
that went with the expectancy. They were happy
and mean when they saw his ill-concealed drunkenness at evening formations, or when he tore up
bunks in the huts, or when he threatened to
court-martial the company as a whole. They were
excited and they waited.

Only in the early mornings did Callan come to
the Orderly room—in the early mornings and at
noon when Swanson was in the mess hall for chow.

The boy would return to find scrawled notes on his desk, instructions for the afternoon work. And now the captain came much more often, pacing nervously about the office, the pencil twining like string between his fingers. He would make as if to check over the boy's work, but the pretense was obvious and it embarrassed them both.

"It's been such a long time since I've checked over this type of thing. But you probably know more about it than anyone. It is correct, isn't it Swanson?"

"Yes sir, I'm sure it is."

"Was Callan—is Sergeant Callan in the habit of checking these things over?"

"Not too thoroughly, sir. It's all pretty pat once you've got it down."

"Ah, fine." Nervously, he moved up and down the room. His face was masked with a preoccupation that quickly dropped when he began to speak. "Frankly, Swanson—" He hesitated, opening and shutting a desk drawer. "I'm disappointed, terribly disappointed."

"Yes sir?"

"Sergeant Callan—he's a fine top sergeant if ever I've seen one." He looked toward the boy for help.

"Yes sir?"

"Sergeant Callan—he's been doing quite a bit of drinking, hasn't he? Yes," he went on, "I'm sure he has. I'm not condemning him, understand, but frankly, Swanson, it worries me. God knows, it's on my mind, yes, certainly it is. It's a bad example

for the men, Swanson. I'm not saying that the
work isn't getting done, understand, but it's not
a good example for the men, and I have my own
position to consider, too." He went to the window
and stared nervously out to the company street.
"It's this damned France, this Quartermaster
Corps. I've seen it happen to a dozen men. I've
seen it get the best of some fine soldiers."
He turned back to the boy as if he were seeking
assurance. "But I've got the company to think of,"
he pleaded, "and my own position."

Callan was living with a woman. It was a rumor
that began in whispers, then crashed upon them
one night when he brought her to the enlisted
men's club. She was a small, frightened, black-
haired girl, and she huddled at one end of the
plank bar without drinking the can of beer he had
bought her. He left her there at the bar and
talked drunkenly with men at one of the tables.
The others in the crowded room watched her. They
could not remember a time when a woman had
been in the bar, but mostly they watched her because she was with the sergeant.

"That's my woman there," he said, pointing
over to the girl, speaking thickly to the group of
men at the table. "Talk to her!" he shouted at the
soldier-bartender. "Try an parley with her," he
demanded. When the embarrassed soldier spoke
a few words of English and then a few of French,
the girl only hung her head and looked at the can
of beer. The sergeant roared with laughter. "She

don't understand anything but Pole!" He surveyed
the room with a wobbly stare. "But she and me
understand each other." He smiled crookedly.
"Plenty good, plenty good!"

Sometimes they saw him driving with the girl
in the Hudson, her small black head barely visible
above the side window. And once or twice she was
seen buying vegetables from peddlers on the road.
They never questioned themselves as to where he
found her. "Ain't no need to think about that,"
scoffed Ivy. "You seen them Polish girls in Bordeaux, them thousan' homeless refoogees."

They could see him driving with her in the evenings, out toward the farmhouse where they lived,
a ramshackle stone house that until a week before
had displayed a "For Rent" sign. Later in the
night he would drive back, bringing her with him
into the heat of the enlisted men's club.

Swanson saw Solange almost every evening. She
owned a Vespa that she drove out on days when it
hadn't rained, meeting him at the crossroads into
Bordeaux after he'd finished work at the camp.
It was the most quiet time of day, toward twilight.
Together they motored over the country roads,
his arms soft around her jacketed waist, the wind
of their motion brushing each side, and when his
arms swelled tighter he could feel the whole flat
warmth of her back and the small closed warmth
of her neck. Coming back he would be driving, and
it was nearly dark now, the vineyards passing
purple and glossy, the wind biting colder, and

suddenly against the night air he could feel the outline of his own chest and the grip of his own hands upon the bars. He could feel it all going forward, and her tucked there behind him with hands across the soft part of his belly and wind-hot cheek pressed to his neck and the breasts touching so graceful on his protected back, and as he felt her and the night and the motion, his back would straighten and arch into her, while joy leaped like a shout into the wind.

It went forward even on the nights alone, in the hut, with the men, the current easier, stronger.

"C'mon Aldous, get that ball and let's toss a few!"

Out onto the gravel street, a soft pass and a clumsy catch, and then another pass as the Negro struggled through the thickness of the gravel.

"C'mon, let's move," cried the boy. "Let's get off this gravel."

They trotted out toward the depot where the ground was harder, passing as they moved, quick passes with feet firm to the ground, quick passes and thumping clean catches in the running twilight.

It was with zest that he would sometimes leave the hut before evening chow, prowling over the countryside, going on foot to explore the same villages where he had drunk with Callan. He wanted to go over those same spots, freely, he wanted to see them new and good. And it was zest that took him one night to the hotel bar in the village of Bernod. He ordered a beer and sandwich and listened to the rolling talk from the next room,

the talk of pimps and hustlers and con men from
Bordeaux, all of them drinking and playing cards
as they waited for the night to deepen toward the
arrival of the soldiers. He was alone. He stood at
the wooden bar eating his sandwich, listening
with pleasure to the voices from the card room.

He was all alone. Then the door behind him
opened and a cold rush of wind swept through the
room. There was no mirror along the bar but somehow he did not need it. He sipped once more from
the beer and when he set it down all the pleasure
was gone and he knew at that moment that no
pleasure could ever last while this could still happen—while his heart was helpless against this quick
and fearful tightening. He did not turn around.
There were three footsteps and the man was beside him.

"You've been following me," said the boy,
hoarsely, almost in a whisper.

"Yeah. Yeah I been following you." And even
in his drunkenness he looked straight at the boy.
The boy stood there and he was sick with knowing
that it could never be right while this could happen. All through himself he was hollow.

"And what if I did? What if I did?" Callan's
face, as he spoke, was a drunken mask. He waited
without expression for the boy to answer. But
as he waited the mask broke and tears flashed into
his eyes and his voice was choked. "You're goddamn rights," he half cried. "I followed you and
I'd follow you again. Oh Christ, boy, boy, understand, understand!" He reached out and clasped

the boy's wrist and his face collapsed into agony.
"I'm feelin rotten, oh Christ, I'm feeling so rotten. God knows I've done things I didn't want to,
but try an understand, that's all I'm asking,
Swans. I'm not a bad guy, I swear I'm not." The
boy stepped back but the hand clutched harder
to his wrist. "Can't you see that nothing like this
ever happened to me before and that you're the
only thing in the whole goddamn world that I
care about? Oh God, God, what I've been through
and how I'm needin you, oh good God," he cried,
and he held fast to the wrist and plunged his head
down into the crook of the boy's arm, and his hat
fell to the floor to show the small gray baldness
at the back of his skull and the short damp hair
that circled it.

He cried into the arm, and the boy, as if para-
lyzed, stared over the empty bar. There was distant
noise from the next room. It made them even more
alone. Slowly, firmly, he pulled his arm away and
then the sergeant peered up and his body still
heaved with sobs. His mouth was full of tears.
"You're never gonna leave me," he said.

The boy stepped back and put his shaking hands
palms downward on the bar and he tried to speak
but his mouth twisted in a dry swallow.

"You ain't gonna leave me ever, 'cause you're
every goddamn thing that counts and you're mine."
He shook himself as if to stop his sobbing and
looked again at Swanson. His face inched toward
the boy.

"No," whispered Swanson. "You're not right!"

For a moment he seemed too choked to go on and he swallowed again and his eyes were dilated with wonder. "I didn't know you could ever talk like that—would be able to."

Callan was no longer crying. His body swayed with a dangerous rhythm and there was rhythm too in each of his soft words. "I gone through hell but I ain't no more. 'Cause you're mine."

"No."

"You're mine."

"It's bad inside you," the boy whispered. He pointed a finger toward the sergeant's chest and he felt that it was a ghostly finger and that the whole world was ghostly. "I see now how bad it's gone," he whispered.

"You can't talk to me, boy. Bad or good! I got so much feeling that nothin makes no difference!"

They both turned to the quick sound of a third person and it was the young waitress who glanced at them and turned back to the other room.

"I'm going," said Swanson. "Don't ever come around me, Sergeant, I'm asking you. Don't come around me!"

"No!" The sergeant's gnarled hand darted out to grab him and finger by finger the boy pried it from his arm. The man's face had whitened into terror and with each grasping breath he said, "No." The boy wheeled around and made for the door. A sharp and terrible cry burst from behind him. "Swanson!"

The man was on him then, one arm around his neck trying to pull him to the floor. "No, no,

Swanson, stay, stay boy, see this, see, see, look!"

Callan's hand was clasping at the boy's body, a clawing hand that squeezed at his shoulder and chest and belly and he felt the hand and his eyes flared wild out to the room and he roared and strained to break loose.

"No!" screamed Callan. "Look! See! See!" The hand clawed at him, at his belly, and as it went down into his crotch the boy roared with lightning strength that came clean as a vision and time was shattered into a white eternity of knowing and shadows were gone forever and the strength ripped its way to the surface and coiled his neck into a muscled whip that cracked the man through the air and crashed him into the wall. The boy was still roaring as he saw him slide down onto the floor. The man was limp and his eyes and mouth were open. He stared up at the boy. "I—I didn't do it! I didn't do nothing!"

The boy was breathing heavily and he was elated as he stared down at the man.

Callan's face was stricken with panic and he did not move from where he'd been thrown. "I swear, I never done anything like that before. Dear God! Dear God!"

The boy stared at him, into the fear and truth of what he said, but it did not matter any longer, and he turned away and walked toward the other room and as he turned the sergeant was up and coming on like a bull. "Swanson!" he screamed.

He was at the door of the card room when the sergeant smashed into him. He went hurtling forward into the room and there was a moment in which he could see the startled faces of the Frenchmen, the card players, the pimps, and then he was crashing into them. And even as he rolled free he could see the quick, murderous hate on the faces of the men who had gone down with him. He tried to locate Callan and he could catch only a glimpse of the khaki uniform hidden back in the doorway. He knew already how it was going to happen and he sprang to his feet and two Frenchmen were off the floor and coming at him. All over the room men were leaping from their chairs, coming toward him. In that last instant he looked once more for the man and he was gone, a terrible and fleeting picture of khaki as it backed into the shadows of the door. He felt a blow square across his mouth and then he was only fighting, catching the first man flush in the neck, hitting the other twice before he went down. There was a moment in which to grab for a chair and he was flailing with it as they swarmed in from every side.

Chapter Twenty-Three

He awoke to see the white ceiling and feel the coarseness, the whiteness of sheets. It came to his mind slowly, easily, that he was in a hospital. He turned his head on the pillow and stared through the window next to his bed. He could see the old familiar green of the meadow. And he could remember all of it and through the remembering he was calm and, strangely, he was happy.

He could feel the bandages pressing tight on his scalp and the effort of turning back from the window caused a quickened throb in his head. He was the only one in the ward. There were four other empty white beds and at the end of the room an Orderly desk that was vacant too. For a time he lay perfectly still in the calm. He knew, with joy, that it was over and ended.

A nurse and a doctor, a first lieutenant, came into the room. They came up to his bed and the young doctor nodded good morning. For a moment he worked over the bandages and when he had them off he bent farther over the bed. "I stitched up some of these cuts last night and I think that's all it'll amount to. You feel all right?"

"I feel good," said Swanson.

The doctor smiled. He straightened up from the bed with a professional briskness. "You were a pretty beat-up soldier when the MPs brought you in. They're going to put that bar off limits."

"Were there any other soldiers picked up there?"

"No. Just you." He stood by the bed. "Your company has been notified, of course. The MPs recommended 'Line of duty' on the Morning Report. They seem to think you were ganged through no fault of your own."

Swanson nodded and he tried to smile and he felt the swollenness of his lips but it did not seem to matter. "When will I be able to leave here?"

The doctor shrugged. "You've got a few days' rest coming."

"I'd like to leave as soon as I can."

The doctor shrugged again and smiled. "To-morrow maybe."

When the doctor left, the nurse stayed to change his bandages. She worked a bit clumsily, talking all the while. "I guess you can tell that I'm new here," she said. She told him that she was a French girl and that she lived in Bordeaux. He asked her if she would take a note for him to Solange. She brought a pencil and paper and he wrote out the note and she promised to deliver it when her shift ended at noon.

He lay quiet all the morning and he did not

have to wonder at the evenness, the goodness of his feeling. He felt it as something deserved, easy, gentle. He lay so that he could look through the window onto the meadow. It was as he'd always seen it, deeply green and sometimes brilliant beneath the sun, but even where it was glittering and brilliant there was that feeling of softness, of sudden collapse. He had never liked to walk through it, through the mist and mystery of hovering insects, and yet he could look at it as he did now and he liked to look at it and know it.

Knowing it made the gentleness. He could see Callan and the man's eyes, those eyes after he was flung into the wall, desperate and blind like a frightened animal's. He could see the hunger in the man, see it vividly, anew, that hunger that was his force. He could think of it and not be afraid. He could think of it now as he lay quiet in the hospital bed, or he could think of it through late and shadowed streets. That desperateness couldn't touch him any more. He knew it. He knew it with the sureness not of a moment but of culmination. And he felt glad that it would be there in his memory, glad for all of it and unashamed.

He lay on the bed looking out into the meadow, and toward noon Aldous Brown came. He could hear the footsteps and he turned and saw him at the door. The Negro waited, and then he came across the room to the bed, slow, tentative. "Hiya, Tom," he said. He looked carefully down at the boy, and then he put a hand on his shoulder and smiled. "Hi, ol' fella." They were both smiling.

"You ain't hurt bad, are yuh?"

"No," he said. "Hell no."

"That sergeant was there, wasn't he?"

"Yes."

"They all know about you being in the hospital. An they know he was in on that thing out there. Them French KPs from Bernod, they were talking at breakfast. They say he made a fight an then run out an let you take it. An when we seen him this morning we knew it was somethin like that. We coulda known, it's funny, we coulda known even without them KPs."

They looked at each other quietly.

"But you is all right, ain't you?"

"Sure I am."

"Thas the important thing," said the Negro. He paused. "An I knew it too. I knew it was all right jus' the minute I stepped in here an seen you." Aldous kept looking at him seriously. He tightened the hand on his shoulder and then he released it. He glanced self-consciously at the floor.

"How is Sergeant Callan?" asked Swanson.

Aldous sat down beside the bed and the black eyes became soft and quiet. "That sergeant been goin crazy, different 'n before, worse 'n before. He come in this mornin terrible drunk an mean, an all mornin he been walkin in that comp'ny street, carryin a bottle in his hand, no tie on or nothin, an I tell you, nobody is comin near him. There ain't nobody in the office, no formations, nothin. Maybe it should be funny but it ain't. Nobody in that comp'ny is laughin."

He looked at Swanson as he spoke. "They say he near killed that Polish girl. This mornin Sergeant Clyde seen her on the road and he say that she was beat up terrible, her face, her face was all bloody. He seen her on the road draggin a suitcase an he try an stop his car an help but she was scared, scared of anybody, an she run off into the fields. He musta beat her after that thing out there. An that man, that sergeant, he probably don't know even that she's gone. All mornin he just been roamin up an down that street. An Cap'n Loring is stayin away. The only thing he done at all was send out to the depot for Cowley. Sent out a note an told him to come in an be clerk. That sergeant, he struck Cowley. He come into the office an seen that boy sitting there an he struck him hard on the face so that that boy come runnin out cryin an scared. Cap'n Loring is stayin away, but he gonna hafta do somethin quick an he know it."

The Negro hesitated and for a moment he did not speak and he placed his hat on his knee and looked at it. "He goin down fast an I ain't heard nobody ask why. We seein it an I guess maybe thas enough. We just waitin, thas all. If it ain't Cap'n Loring, some man from Post is gonna come put that sergeant away."

He paused again. "They watch that man an they is scared, an even more 'n that, they is sad. Can you know what I'm sayin? They hate that man, an they been hatin him for months. But always he was

a soldier an they knew it. Now he like a wild animal
an they see it an it give 'em that sad feelin."

He looked at Tom, hesitant, as if it had been
wrong to speak of it. "Can you know what I
mean?"

The boy raised himself slightly in the bed, serious. "Yes. Sure I know, I do."

For a while they sat without speaking. Aldous
stood up, putting his cap on carefully. "I'll be
comin back. Maybe tonight I'll be comin back."

"That's good. I'll be waiting for you."

Aldous stood for a few moments longer by the
bed. His eyes brightened some, happy, almost in
wonder. "An you is all right," he said.

In the middle of the afternoon he heard the
approach of her high-heeled shoes. Her face, when
he saw her at the doorway, was delicate, pink. They
watched each other and as she stood there everything about her, her skin, the tilt of her body,
seemed expectant.

"I'm not hurt a bit," he said.

She came over beside the bed with tears already
starting, tears that ran freely without contorting
her face. "You are hurt." Her voice was thick with
its effort at restraint. He reached out and brought
her close, and he knew he could laugh or cry, either
one, and it would all come from the same goodness. He kissed her cheeks, the wetness of them,
holding her close. "Oh God, you good girl, you
good, good girl." Her hand was on his chest over

the hot damp hospital shirt, her lips were kissing his neck, and her hand pressed his chest as if to caress the warm and living openness. "It's all good there," he whispered.

"Oh Tom, I can feel it." She moved slowly back, sitting there on the edge of the bed, and the color of her face was so high and yet so thin he thought he could see into her. "I can feel it, I can tell, oh Tom, I hope it's not wrong but I'm happy, I'm so happy."

"This happened with Callan, you know that don't you?"

"I know, yes."

He looked at the high color of her. "There's a lot I won't have to tell you."

She smiled, shaking her head.

But he told her of the night before He told her of Callan's following him to the bar, of his tears, his desperateness, of his hands reaching, clutching. "It almost had to happen." He spoke slowly. "It was almost inevitable. And when it happened it was a kind of freedom, a kind of end."

He told her of the fight afterward.

And then they waited, thinking of it together.

"Where is he now?" she asked.

"And that's it," he said. "It doesn't matter. It'll never matter where he is."

She stayed by his bed through the afternoon, and he touched her often and he could touch even the hardness of her cheekbones and it would excite him. He kissed her often and she was close so that her heart moved against his chest and he felt opened up into her, his heart expanding all through her, and no longer was the ring there, the ring around his heart. He told her again and again, "God, oh God, how I love you." And she answered by pressing closer and he knew that it was growing, building, and that it would never stop.

She stayed until dark, and toward dark Aldous Brown came back. He shook Solange's hand, warmly, and yet there was an urgency about him. He took a chair by the bed and he began almost at once to speak, and as he began his voice slipped out of its thickness and he spoke in a way that Swanson had never heard him. He talked with his chin slightly raised, his eyes steady on the opposite wall, and his voice was clear with an inspiration that was so steady it seemed almost considered.

"He called us out to a formation. It was at dusk time, just a while ago. He was there in front and he had no shave and his eyes were red and his uniform dirt all over and torn too. He was starting to tell us something. Captain Loring came down the sidewalk and said loud that he was relieving him of his duties as first sergeant. Said it right there in front of us all. Sergeant Callan, he turned and looked at the captain and there was just quiet in that whole company street. He said real quiet that his name was Master Sergeant Albert Callan and that he never in his life been relieved from a duty. He said that if he was going to be relieved from

duty that it was no man like Captain Loring who
was to do it. And he stood up there square to that
captain and he said that just the way the captain
held himself showed what kind of man he was,
and that if he was gonna come up to him in front
of his men that he would come like an officer and
a soldier, not like what he was. Then he called
the captain every name. He called him weak and he
kept telling him to stand up, to put back his shoulders and look like an officer and a man. The captain
couldn't do nothing. His face was like he was gonna
cry. Everybody just went away from the formation.
Silent-like. Everybody watched from the huts.
Them two men were all alone there on the sidewalk. The sergeant kept at him, he made him do
it, we all seen, the captain was standing up there
at attention."

The Negro lowered his head. "Just a while ago
that was. Sergeant Callan, he still around there.
Everybody's just sitting in the huts. Everybody's just
sitting there, and Lord, it's a funny feeling in that
company."

There was a long quiet between the three of
them.

"Somethin's going to happen," said Aldous.

In the morning he asked to be released and the
doctor consented. His only clothes were those he
had been admitted in, the blood-stained khakis.
He dressed beside his bed, and as he knotted the
tie he could feel the stiffness of his collar, the

bloodiness. Before he left the ward he looked at himself in the mirror. The blood was dry and brown all across the front of his shirt. He went down the corridor to pick up his release papers, and through the rows of windows he could see the yellow brilliance of the morning.

And the sergeant watched the morning sun.

It came through a crack in the Orderly room door, a yellow rod across the floor. He inched the door closed, watching the rod become thin, and then he made it fatter and then once again he made it thin. Then slowly he closed the door, choking the line until it was gone. Without looking out he could still hear the sound of approaching vehicles. He could hear and feel them as they approached and passed.

Carefully, he turned and looked once more at the clock above the file cabinet. It showed eight-thirty. He watched the clock and then his gaze slid down the file cabinet, down to the circle of cigarette butts on the dusty floor, the dried spittle, the imprint in the dust of where he had slept. He gazed slowly over the room, and with the same slowness his tongue went across the front of his teeth. With two or three strange steps he moved to his desk and picked up a partially filled whisky bottle. He took one swallow. He lowered his arm and let it fall from his hand onto the floor.

Outside, the street was empty and the sun slanted down into it so that the gravel was dry and almost sparkling. No one had left the company, yet the street was without movement and the hut doors were closed.

Sergeant Callan came out of the Orderly room and started down the wooden sidewalk. His walk was tight and paced and then he broke for a few feet into a loping trot, only to catch himself and slow. He was bareheaded, the thin, short-cut hair damp and matted to his head, and his khaki shirt hung loosely outside his belt, yet even beneath the looseness his back curved full and strong. Two or three times he trotted, anxious uncertain bursts. Mostly he went stiff-legged and with care. He knew that they were watching, there in the huts, there behind the closed doors.

At the weapons hut he stopped and he unlocked the door from a ring of keys and closed it behind him. In the cool and darkened smell of steel and oil he paused. He could listen to the beat of his heart. The ring of keys was soft in his palm. He unlocked the rack of M-1 rifles and he took one rifle and then opened the shell cabinet on the wall and took out a clip and forced it down into the chamber. For a moment, in the dark room, he held the rifle at waist level. When he stepped outside into the sun he kept himself still and felt the touch of each window of each hut. Then he broke into a slow run, out through the softness of the meadow, carrying the weapon tightly in one hand.

He ran through the meadow out toward the woods and when he came into the shelter of the trees he slowed and tried to ease his breathing.

He lurched against the trunk of a tree and his eyes fell and hung on the leaf-covered earth. He stood there for a moment as if bewildered, as if he did not know what he was about. From his throat began a little humming sound, high-pitched, even, and his eyes widened and seemed to roam for its source. For an instant the woods were perfectly still. And then he began the sound again, listening with wide eyes as it grew, listening as it grew and humped itself into a single, lilting sob. "Oh, good Lord above." His hand loosened until the rifle nearly dropped from it. "Good Lord above," he whispered, and he let the rifle fall against his leg and put his face to the tree.

Through the woods it was soft and padded and windless. The sun slipped barely through the trees. The sergeant kept as still as the woods. And then he lifted his head and his eyes seemed suddenly radiant. His face began to grow with color. "Like that! Yes," he whispered. "Yes, yes." He turned, frantically as if to search his direction through the trees. His voice was half pleading and yet there was gold in it too. "He'll be there, good Lord, I'll find him good Lord."

He took up the weapon and began running just inside the fringe of trees, parallel to the meadow. He ran without slowing until he could see the meadow begin to narrow and then he dropped to his knees and crawled to the edge of the wood. From where he was he could look across at the hospital. He stayed on his knees. His head was tilted, his neck bent nearly into his shoulder.

"I'll see him," he prayed. "He'll come out of there, good Lord."

For some moments he waited. Once, with a hand that was hysterical and almost separate, he tucked his flopping shirt beneath his pants belt. He waited in the terrible slow passing of time.

Across the meadow the door of the hospital opened and the boy came out. The sergeant saw him and flushed and nearly cried. "See," he whispered. "Oh yes, yes."

He watched the boy start down the steps of the hospital and as he raised himself into a crouch the beat of his heart seemed nearly to shake his balance. Slowly, carefully, he advanced into the open glare of the meadow. "Haaaaa . . ." he called. It was a call like the short roughness that scatters a stray dog. "Haaaa. . . . Haaaaaaa!"

He saw the boy stop on the steps and search for the sound, and he knew when the boy had seen him, knew by the sudden stiffness of the distant figure. "Yes, yes," he murmured, a beginning ecstasy. That boy would see, that boy would know, he was going to know! He held the rifle above his head, visible, shaking it, and once again he made the call. "Haaaa!" For a second he waited, two seconds, and then he turned, running back toward the wood. He ran and he whispered, "He's there, he's there, he'll know now, good Lord."

His legs began to lose their heaviness and his rifle became light, part of his running self, and his thoughts seemed to rise until they were as smooth and flowing as his body. He ran fast, faster.

In the flashing of the trees there was the coming of the rise. He was sure now, sure. He was going to come up into it, into the high rareness, into the peaked moments. The peaked moments, there had been peaked moments. And he ran faster to have them back again, all together, all at once. It was as life was meant, packed together, no emptiness between, all packed and choking full. And the wood was a swirling green motion. And he ran now with his glories bunched so wonderfully painful and his breath was a whisper in the wind. "He's with me, I've got him, I've got him now." And faster through the trees he ran and the pain grew wonderfully and it had to go on, higher and higher, and his head leaned out to skip against the bark of trees and the blood came warm down his face. Through the trees was a green clearing. A little green clearing ahead. He saw it and the feeling rose, screamed, and there was that last bursting sureness as he plunged into the clearing, leaping out toward the earth.

And on the earth, beneath the blue sky, he became so quiet and so wickedly graceful, and gracefully, lightly, he rolled upon his back. He turned the rifle around toward himself and his thumb reached just to the trigger and the weapon was light and like a musical instrument, a flute or a horn, and it was so terrible and divine beneath the stare of the barrel, for he had hardly any body, only the islands of his navel and heart and the gentle throbbing between his eyes. Ever so slowly, the barrel moved and lingered over each of the islands. And then he raised one knee slightly into the air. He put the barrel to the heat of his heart.

The report of the rifle rang through the country-side. The boy closed his eyes, lightly. He was standing on the hospital steps. He closed his eyes and waited while his body caught and tightened with the intensity, the sorrow of it. The echo of the report hung alive like a current, the only sound. It held him, shrunk him. And then he opened his eyes and it passed. Men were running through the morning sun toward the wood. He turned away from it and went down the steps, and as he walked it was suddenly very quiet, a quiet like the listening of dawn, and he could hear the farthest sounds, and as he walked he breathed deeply and his breathing was steady and clear.